novum ⬤ pro

AF280281

Bee Grey

A Mixed Bag

novum pro

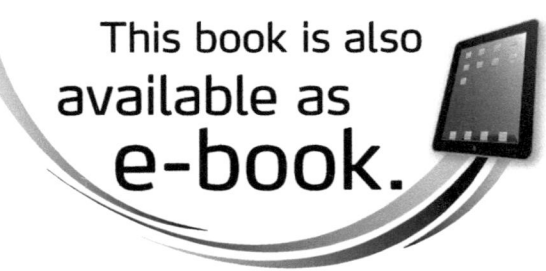

This book is also available as e-book.

www.novum-publishing.co.uk

All rights of distribution, including via film, radio, and television, photomechanical reproduction, audio storage media, electronic data storage media, and the reprinting of portions of text, are reserved.

Printed in the European Union on environmentally friendly, chlorine- and acid-free paper.

© 2020 novum publishing

ISBN 978-3-99064-795-0
Editing: Ashleigh Brassfield
Cover photo:
Ihor Smishko | Dreamstime.com
Cover design, layout & typesetting:
novum publishing

www.novum-publishing.co.uk

Tormented

I watched them arguing. Not a pretty sight, him towering over her, and her stretching up to her full height, coming only to his shoulders despite the six-inch heels she was wearing. His eyes dark with anger, he stared at her as he mouthed his obscenities.

I watched her shoulders slump as her face registered disbelief that such foul language was on his otherwise gentle tongue. Her eyes seemed to ask 'Who is this man?' Obviously not the man she thought, by the look on her face as she pulled herself together, though her fists remained clenched. Her language remained clean, though you could easily see the anger that sparkled in her fiery blue eyes. She repeatedly tossed her sandy hair over her shoulder and brushed the full fringe out of her eyes.

Suddenly, without warning, she turned from him intending to walk away. He reached out with his long arms pulling her back tight into him, kissing her hard on the mouth. She struggled, pushing her hands against his chest without any real effect. When he released his hold she staggered backwards a step or two glaring at him, then wiped her lips with the sleeve of her navy blouse, turning again in fury to walk briskly to a red convertible parked some yards away. The driver of the car, wearing sunglasses and a white T-shirt, pushed the door open as she approached, having the car on the move as she buckled her seat belt. She did not look back at him.

He stood watching them drive away rubbing the back of his head in disbelief. His anger not abated, he slapped a nearby wall in frustration, bending this way and that like a tree in cross winds. The anger slowly began to weaken, leaving his now white face looking something akin to sorrowful mourning. He staggered to a bench watching the road, waiting, hoping, for an hour or more.

Finally, standing slowly, he walked to a pub ordering a pint, taking it to an outside table where he could observe the passing traffic. He sighed deeply, his drink mostly untouched. After a couple of hours, leaving half a glass of beer on the table, he left the pub, striding to the park close by, where he trudged round the paths, not seeing the beautiful roses nor enjoying their perfume. He proceeded without observing, past the shrubbery where small birds hid out of the hot sun, then past the hot houses with their canna lilies outside, unaware of their beautiful colours. Continuing down the path, he finally stopped near the bandstand, where an enthusiastic brass band was playing in the glorious sunshine, while birds, defeated in their songs, listened reluctantly in the trees, looking down at the people sheltering in the shade below.

He stood staring at the band, taking time to register where he was. Eventually slumping down on the grass, as many others had, put his hands behind his head and closed his eyes to the sun to let the brass band's tunes wash over him. There he lay for the hour and a half that the band continued to play, rising only as a tin was rattled nearby him. Getting up, he took some coins out of his pocket, dropping them in the tin before slowly, with sunken shoulders and head bent towards the ground, he returned back to the garden entrance, towards home.

Arriving home to the flat they had shared, now empty not only of her things but of her spirit, her essence gone, he walked slowly from room to room. He touched doors that she had touched, lingered in her favourite chair, though he could not settle there. Later he found a scarf of hers left lying under a stool. He picked it up, stroking it in his large hands before lifting it to his face to smell the scent of her. He picked up a book she had left on the bed. A book, she had read, a self-help book she had suggested he should read too.

Taking a seat by the window, he opened the book. He read a paragraph, stood up to wander round the flat, before sitting to read some more. This was how he spent the rest of the day and most of the night. He finally lay on their bed in the early hours in a cold deep sleep. He shuddered a number of times as his dreams tormented him. Waking the following morning he showered, dressed, ate a slice of toast before going to work, as normal. As he worked, he thought about the book she had left. Perhaps there was some truth in it all.

On his way home he passed a church, going in for a few minutes to its comforting smell of incense, the dim eternal light offering a glimmer of hope. The church was mostly lit through the stained glass windows. Taking a seat in the shadows at the back of the church, he watched, finding some solace at the quiet movement of the priests and parishioners as they went about their business. The calm settled him, returning him to a semblance of the man he thought he should be, though regretting the man of yesterday. Slowly, he stood, bowed his head and with a lighter step returned to his home with a quieter mind.

I noticed over the next few weeks his routine was to go there after work, sitting in the quiet of the church where occasionally a priest came to sit by him, sometimes in companionable silence, occasionally speaking gently to him and his tormented soul. Always he went home alone to cook a light supper before going to bed, sleeping uneasily till morning. After several months, as an elderly priest sat beside him, as he came to the conclusion he really did not belong in the outside world.

Finally, he spoke of his anguish in hushed tones. He told of the girl who had tormented him and finally took him with her. Speaking with mixed emotions, he told of his journey into factory work and the trials of the work place, while she started to torment him, wanting more than he could give. He spoke of the evening classes he undertook to improve his chances of a more rewarding life, of giving her a better future; of her previously unknown arrangement with a wealthy man who could give her everything she desired.

Eventually, with tears, he told of all he had left behind. The love. The comradeship. The quiet laughter and the learning. His desertion for a girl whose empty wishes he could not fulfil. What a fool he had been. Then the tears finally fell while raking sobs shook his now slightly undernourished body.

When the tears subsided, along with the sobs, he looked into the priest's face for the first time. 'I do not belong here,' he wrung his hands, his whole body seeming to move, agitating, bowed under a grief he could no longer contain, 'but how can I go back now?' The elderly priest took his hand taking him to the private dining room at the rear of the church. He quietly garnered more details of his previous life, while plying him with a light supper of cold cuts with mashed potatoes containing a medley of vegetables.

Two hours later, he was accompanied by two priests back to his flat, one to sleep in a chair while the other, looked round the flat, before returning to his office in the church to make some phone calls.

Waking the following morning to the smell of coffee, I watched as he mentally ran through the previous evening. He showered, dressed and entered the small kitchen where the priest, Richard, was busy making toast and boiled eggs to go with the coffee. He smiled weakly at him as he served him breakfast. Richard asked what his plans were. 'I have a contract to work, people are relying on me. I must finish what I have started. I will also think about whether to go back to my old life. I cannot keep swapping one for another. If I go back, if they will have me, I need to be sure it is right for me and for them.' They parted company, one to the priest's house, the other to his place of work, where a quieter, more stable person emerged.

I watched as he contemplated all the hurdles he had yet to jump over. I saw his inner strength return; his back began to straighten, his face began to soften. He no longer barked at those below him, but took them to his office speaking softly while listening with understanding to their own problems.

After a couple of months, I stood silently at his shoulder as he handed in his month's notice. He wrote a letter to his ex-girl friend apologising for his erratic behaviour, saying the flat would be empty within a fortnight, and he had paid the rest of the rent till the contract ran out in three months' time. At the end of the month, packing his few belongings, he left a final note with her scarf before closing the door gently behind him.

I stood, watching, as he said farewell to the priests thanking them for their guidance. The old priest accompanied him to the station, speaking kindly before he climbed onto the train with trepidation, the train back to the monastery where he had been living five years ago, not knowing if he would still be accepted. He had finally come to realise that it was as a monk he served his god best. Arriving at the monastery in the twilight of a summer evening, he was surprised as he approached the door, it swung open. The abbot came down the steps to welcome back him with open arms, his face alight with obvious joy. With the abbot's arm on his shoulder they entered the monastery, chatting like old friends.

Two Bowls of Soup
and a Ride in a Police Car

I arrived at my Tai Chi session fairly relaxed. It was 'me time', time to leave the world's worries behind and concentrate on me. I wrongly believed that having 'me time' was selfish; how I wish I had given up this foolish notion years ago. 'Family first' was always the mantra in my household. A lot of good that did me. Looking back over the years, 'family first' always got in the way of 'me time', a time needed to grown and assess, but not anymore.

It takes me 20–30 minutes to walk to my class; it largely depends on how tired I am. It takes most of those 20 minutes to get my head into thinking about Tai Chi instead of my daily issues. Having a leg injury, Tai Chi is one of the few exercise classes I can do without any worries. I walk in to find about half a dozen people already there, chatting about their week.

We are mostly an older group, though recently four younger ladies joined us. There are five men in the group of twelve who turn up each week. We are a motley group; most are retired, though not all. One teaches a different type of exercise class, one works as a part time receptionist, another and his cheerful wife are photographers traveling the world in the hope of getting 'the one photo', a special photo to put their names on the world stage. Their wedding photography as well as portraits of animals and people keep them busy.

Those who do not work have an interesting array of hobbies. One is in a photography group, another a gardener. A lovely lady called Cath and her husband like visiting local towns, spending the day looking at the latest in the shops, walking through the parks and so on. Sandra is on call to look after her new grandchild. As her son lives far away, it usually means a week or two at a time going to stay with them. Brett whose wife comes ad hoc to the group due to charity commitments, have a caravan and toddles off as and when to visit this member of the family or another, sometimes travelling quite long distances fitting in friends along the way. Knitting, craft groups and bridge groups are also common interests.

A lovely couple of a similar age to myself also have a caravan. They enjoy their holidays across Europe, frequently meeting up with friends at camp sites to share news.

Cath, a short lady with a gorgeous smile, shouts out 'Hello!' followed by 'What have you been up to this morning?'

'Making soup,' I reply.

'Making soup... is it worth the effort?'

'Absolutely, there is nothing so warming as homemade soup.'

'What kind of soup did you make?'

'Butternut squash, my absolute favourite, though I have been told it is one of the worse the waistline.'

'Why is that?' Jake chimes in.

'Apparently the starch in it turns rapidly to sugar, so I don't make it too often. Then I made a sprout soup.'

A loud chorus of 'Sprout soup?' A silence fell, though it did not last for long.

Pat asked, 'Does it taste alright?'

I laugh. 'Yes, it does, much better than I thought it would, though I did add some chicken bones to the soup, straining them out when cooked, just so the meat left on the bones would give it some protein.' I reflect for a moment or two. 'I guess you could add cheese, but I don't because I am lactose intolerant.'

Our tutor, a lovely young man with lots of knowledge about the body, calls us to start the class. We work on a new Tai Chi exercise.

As I leave Cath asks me to wait a moment. Outside the hall she tells me that Peter's partner died last Thursday. She only mentioned it as the two groups that Peter runs has been cancelled for a couple of weeks.

I walk home with Peter and his lovely partner Gavin on my mind. I have a great admiration for Peter. They were so very close, both so different. Two halves of a whole. They have been through such a lot together and both are generous with their time, being involved in many groups, just to share what they have or raise funds for local charities.

Arriving home, I find the delicious smell of soup lingering in the air. I had left them out to cool so some could be frozen to eat at a later date. I rummage round the cupboards for two suitable containers pouring a different soup into each one before putting them in a convenient bag to carry. As Peter lives not five minutes' walk from me, I am soon knocking on his door.

A very pale, unfocused Peter answers the door.

'I am so sorry Peter; I've just heard. You must be absolutely devastated, how are you coping?' Peter opens the door wider to let me enter. 'I hope you don't mind,' I say as I look round at the flowers festooning the house, 'I brought you some homemade soup. I thought you might not want the bother of cooking all the time for yourself. Each can be used as a main meal or split if you want just a snack.'

We have walked into the kitchen, strange, really, as I have not been in there before. The kitchen is tidy with a tray set for tea, complete with a couple of scones, butter and jam. I put the two soups on the countertop.

'When did you eat last?' I ask Peter, who shrugs his shoulders. I give him a big hug as the tears swell in his pale blue eyes and his light beard rests on my head. My hands stay wrapped around his waist for a good few minutes.

We both prefer coffee, so when Peter releases me I put the kettle on, asking him where the coffee and cups are. Soon we are in his study, where Peter tells me that Gavin just collapsed in his beloved garden.

'The ambulance seemed to take an age to get here, but it wasn't really that long. I stayed at the hospital with him, though I wasn't allowed in the resus. unit. Eventually they moved Gavin to a side ward. It appeared he'd had a massive heart attack.' Peter pauses, his shoulders slumped and shuddering. I hold his hand with my left hand, giving him a tissue with the other. When Peter has settled, he continues. 'They couldn't do anything for him.'

Silence enveloped us. The ticking of a distant clock could be heard, unusual in today's world of digital clocks. Peter suddenly said, 'It belonged to his mother.'

'Pardon?'

'The clock you can hear.' A sniff and a shudder, though this one was less violent. 'We only had it repaired a couple of months ago. It was his pride and joy, left to him in his mother's will...'

I look round Peter's study. It is as I remember it. Always so very tidy, the opposite of mine which seems to be littered with a multitude of things I'm 'working on.' We met at a local club for retirees some ten years ago. Peter's group was one of the first I went to. Other opportunities arose, but not before I learned to admire Pete and Gavin, who were generous with their time outside of clubs and groups.

Peter broke into my thoughts. 'How did you hear?'

'I met Cath at Tai Chi. I wanted to say how sorry I was and let you know I'm thinking of you.' I watch him as he unfolds out of his seat to his full height, towering above me even when I'm standing. 'I'll come back another day.' I lead the way to the front door then turn back to face him. 'Peter, I only live just round the corner, let me know when the funeral is and if you need any help, even if only for washing up.'

Peter nods his head. I open the door to walk down the garden to the front gate. The door is already closed as I turn to put the catch on the gate, to stop the light wind blowing it open.

Walking to the gym on the following Monday in a colder wind, I am glad I have put on my colourful jacket, one I had bought for a special occasion some twelve years before in a little boutique in Nottingham. The background is dark mauve, with various triangles in red, green, blue and yellow. It is much envied, with plenty of offers to 'throw it in my direction when you are finished with it,' met only with smiles from me.

A steady stride of twenty minutes usually takes me to the gym, my warm up time, I remind myself, as a Police patrol car pulls up a few yards in front of me. Two officers get out, one to stand in front of me.

'Excuse me madam,' the younger officer said. 'Would you mind coming with us for a chat?'

'Why, what have I done wrong? I am on my way to the gym!'

'Probably nothing at all, we just need you at the station to answer a couple of questions.'

He pauses as his mate continues, 'We'll drop you off at the gym once we have had a chat.' His face focuses enquiringly on mine.

I look at him for some moments, then look towards the way to the gym. I look at the police car where the second officer, slightly taller, is standing by the open rear door. I look from one to the other, then reluctantly walk to the car.

I am soon seated in an interview room. The taller officer asks if I would like a cup of tea.

Grumpily, I reply, 'Coffee with alternative milk and one sweetener please.'

'Don't think I can do alternative milk madam.' I dive into my sports bag, just an old favourite carry bag, bringing out a small milk flask.

'Good job I brought my own then. So it'll be black coffee, I've already sweetened the milk.'

They both smile at me. With one standing by the door the other leaves to make my coffee, or to get someone else to make a coffee. He returns with a paper cup of black coffee, complete with a spoon and a couple of wrapped sweeteners.

I smile my thanks, adding some of my milk then sipping the coffee. How I hate drinking out of paper cups. I just cannot abide the taste of cardboard. Plastic is worse though. Having taken a sip, I ask, 'So what is the reason I am here?'

'Just a moment madam, someone from C.I.D wants to interview you.'

'Why?'

'Just a formality. They will be about ten minutes.'

'Could I use a loo then?' I am given strange looks. 'Look, the first thing I do when I get to the gym is spend a penny, I had walked most of the way there when you two asked me to join you. Now, if I am to wait for someone else, I need a loo, or you might need a mop!'

I accompany a cheerful, fair-haired female officer to a cloak room. We speak about the gym and how long I had been going there, just incidentals. We chat on the way back to the interview room to find my coffee had a plain clothes officer to keep it company. He stood, held out his hand.

'Sorry to ask you to come in, we just need some clarification. My name is Sergeant Platt, please sit down, your coffee is cool enough to drink now. What milk is that you put into the coffee?'

'Almond milk. I am lactose intolerant and also have a slight intolerance to soy, so I drink almond milk most of the time.'

'Is it any good?'

'Yes, if you like milk in your coffee as I do.'

I sit down opposite Sergeant Platt. The lady officer who had accompanied me takes a seat besides mine. 'Would you like some biscuits?' she asks with smiling, deep blue eyes.

I return her smile. 'Thank you for the offer. I'm also a celiac so most grains are excluded. It's a bind, but I feel so much better without the gluten. I've shrunk a dress size, so it is right for me' I turn to face Sergeant Platt. 'So are you going to tell me why my day has been interrupted? As far as I am aware, I have not done anything wrong and cannot think what information I could have that would interest you.'

Sergeant Platt appears slightly amused. 'Your name is?' He has a pen poised over a sheet of paper headed with the station name.

I sigh. 'My name is Karen Davis and I live in the court at the top of Victoria Drive.'

'What were you doing at 3 Courton Close last Wednesday, at about five?'

'Visiting a friend who had lost his partner. I took him a couple of bowls of soup he could warm up. I made us both coffee, we sat and chatted for about an hour, then I left to go home.'

'Do you have a key to the property?'

'No,' I raise my hands in supplication. 'Why would I? Although I have great admiration for Peter, we were not close enough for him to give me a key. Yes, I do look at his Facebook page and sometimes make comments, but that is about it.' I fall silent taking several sips of coffee. 'I also go to some of his fundraising events, if they are on when I am free.' I cross my legs, letting my left leg swing a bit then putting my foot back on the floor. 'Why am I here?'

'You were seen at the house. Someone thought you had gone inside. The family found two bowls of soup inside when they visited and wanted to know how they arrived there.' He looked at me from under dark eyebrows. 'Are you sure you don't have a key?' My left hand goes into my left trouser pocket pulling out my keys. 'Take them and check out my house then Peter's house. I assure you I do not have a key to Peter's home. As I said, **we** are acquaintances rather than friends, close or otherwise.'

'You see Karen, Peter died the day after his partner Gavin. No one has been in the house apart from family. So, we would like to know how you managed to put two bowls of soup in the house?'

I freeze. My mind stills. I stare at him. The coffee cup starts to drop out of my hand, caught by Sargent Platt. An arm comes round my shoulders. I begin to feel, feel dazed, my head starts to spin. I put my head in my hands, wiping them down my face. I look back at where Sargent Platt was sitting, but he has moved to my left side. He picks up my left hand. His hand feels hot on mine. I turn to him.

'Are you seriously telling me,' I pause, trying to compute, 'Are you seriously telling me I knocked on a door. A ghost let me in the house. I made coffee for two. I left two bowls of soup in the kitchen. I hugged a ghost. *I hugged a ghost?*' I start to stand up, but a firm hand pushes me back down.

Sargent Platt stands up, to be replaced by a doctor from my local surgery. Suddenly I have my blood pressure taken, my heart listened to. All the while I keep repeating, 'I was let in by a ghost. A ghost. Ghosts can't do that, can they?' I look at the doctor. 'They can't, can they?'

He gently replies, 'I think they can, unless we can find a better explanation.' He leaves the interview room and returns a few minutes later, picking up my keys from the table. 'Come, I will take you home. Is there anyone there?'

'No, just me. I think I'll give the gym a miss today. I'll make a hot drink and lie down for an hour or so.'

Doctor Swift takes me home making sure I'm OK before he leaves. Turning at my door, he asks, 'I'll ask one of our nurses to visit around six, is that ok?'

I nod, and forget the drink, going straight to my bedroom. I draw the curtains and snuggle under the duvet. 'A ghost let me in.' I remain in bed for several hours before getting up on shaky legs to warm a bowl of soup to have with a (gluten free) bread roll. The nurse rings the doorbell as I am washing up.

'Hi Karen, Doctor Swift asked me to call. That's a lovely smell,' she sniffs the air again, 'smells like pumpkin soup.'

'Would you like some?'

'Yes, but I'd better not. Hubby's cooking tonight and he'll be offended if I leave my dinner. Thanks for the offer though.' She looks at me, checking my colour, my heart rate and blood pressure. 'Well, you look fine. Doctor Swift has made an appointment at the end of the week for you. Please keep it.'

I open up my iPad while Nurse Brown packs up her bag. I open Facebook, where there is a message for me. It reads: 'Thank you for the soup. Such a kind thought.'

I mutter, 'Nooo.' Nurse Brown comes up behind me. 'Look, look, it's from Peter. Sent... sent... twenty minutes ago!'

She looks at the time and reads the message. We look at each other, then both watch, mesmerised, as the message erases itself.

If Only

He stood there, straight backed, arms hanging by his sides, but his fists were clenched. His lightly bearded chin stuck out slightly. He rocked lightly back and forth, like a soft summer breeze that barely touches. He gazed straight ahead, noticing only the thoughts in his head. The woman in front of him, slim with auburn hair and a good head shorter than he was, watched the slight waves of emotion flickering over his face. She took a small step back from him, her eyes remaining on his face. Then she took a step to the side, noticeable only if you were watching. Several small sideways steps followed, then she turned to walk away from him. Suddenly his hand shot out, stopping her. She turned to look at him. He was still looking forward.

'Why Sally, why?' he asked in a loud whisper. 'Is what we have not enough? What more can I give you.'

'I have just told you,' was the reply.

'No, that was not a reason.' He finally turned his head to look into her soft brown eyes. 'I need a proper reason, not a list of excuses.' He studied her face. 'If there is someone else, fair enough. If I have done something you cannot forgive, I'll try to live with that too. All you have given me is a list of excuses.' He paused, breathing heavier than before. 'I feel used. Dirty. You have taken everything from me.' His eyes wandered over her slight form. 'Do you know what you want? I mean, what you truly want, or is life a game? Fleece the guy and walk away laughing with your mates.'

She noticed the tears forming in his pale blue eyes. Saw the quiver of his chin, so slight, but there. She felt his hand fall away from her but remained turned towards him. For the first time in her life she felt a sadness engulf her. A feeling new to her, a feeling she had only read about in books. Finally, she pulled her eyes away from his but remained where she stood. Her eyes now on the concrete ground she stood on.

'Have I just used him?' she asked herself. There was no answer. She walked slowly away, leaving him half turned to watch as she crossed the road.

Ten years to the day, Sally returned to the same spot. She stood tall, slim and graceful in black heels, black stockings, and wearing a black suit of skirt with matching jacket with a pale blue blouse under it. Her work clothes. She was successful; a good job in a large buying department, good money, her own home in a nice area. In fact, she had everything she could possibly want, except what she wanted most: the man she left here ten years ago.

The area looked similar. One or two shops looked a little more tired, others had bright fronts and gleaming interiors. A new coffee bar had opened, bright red office chairs round gleaming glass tables, waiters in dark trousers, black shoes, white soft shirts and bow ties. 'Wow. This is a change.' She crossed the silent road going into the café, impressed by the soft lighting away from the windows. Her eyes took in the elegant counter, with cakes, sandwiches, salads and more. 'Hmm,' she murmured to herself 'it all looks very impressive.'

A waiter asked where she would like to sit. 'Near a window, but not obviously seen from outside.' He suggested a table, leading her to it and ensuring she was seated comfortably. She looked out the window, watching the spot she had last seen him. 'This is ridiculous,' she told herself. The waiter left her a menu, with a separate sheet for today's 'special offers.' Picking up the menu, she opted for a double espresso with a spot of milk and a slice of chocolate cake with pure fruit cream, ordered from an older waiter whose soft brown hair fell lightly over his face.

When he returned with her order, she smiled her thanks. Picking up her espresso she sipped it as she watched the street. Half an hour later she ordered another espresso, her cake remaining untouched. This was how she spent her afternoon, watching everyone who walked over that spot. As the day started to turn to dusk, her shoulders began to slump. The streetlights began to turn on. The day that had started bright and sunny had turned to rain as did her hopes.

As she decided to leave, two ladies she recognised arrived to sit at a table slightly away from her. 'Mark's neighbours,' she whispered to herself. Relaxing back in her seat she picked at the remnants of the sandwich she had ordered half an hour ago.

With bags falling this way and that, the two ladies studied the menu on the table. 'I think I'll have a prawn sandwich today. Gosh my feet feel sore.' The larger lady, in a brown woven coat, green scarf wound round her neck, removing her matching brown hat to reveal steel grey hair said, 'Marge, we've walked all day, never had a lunch time sit.' She eyed the bags surrounding them. 'Looking at that lot you would think we were shopping for the whole street.

'Do you think we over did it then, Vera?' They looked at each other bursting into laughter.

An older waiter came over for their order. 'Mine's a cheese and pickle, Marge is having a prawn sandwich,' looking at Marge, she continued, 'Hot chocolate as usual?'

Marge nodded. 'Shouldn't really, my feet have enough weight to carry as it is... Still, we don't come out often, do we?'

Vera shook her head. 'Just as well looking at this lot, it'll take till next Christmas to pay for it all.'

Their coffee and sandwiches arrived, and the pair gratefully tucked in. After a few minutes, Vera said, 'Shame about the Potters though, did you hear?

'No, tell all!'.

'Well you know his wife died?' Marge nodded her head as she took another bite of prawn sandwich. 'Well, he was taken ill. Peter, their son, moved him closer to him. His wife was a rock, by all accounts.' Vera stopped to eat a bite of her cheese and pickle sandwich. Continuing, she said, 'They have three children, you know; eventually took him into their home to give proper care to him. Not many lasses would do that!' Vera took another bite of her sandwich. 'He died a week or two ago. They say Peter is devastated, had to take time off work.'

Marge interrupted her flow. 'Still, he has a good lass with him now, not like that Sally he mooned over all those years ago. She would have been useless. He was well rid of her.'

'No, you mustn't talk like that about her. She loved him as much as he loved her. Wrote regular but his mother tore up the letters and burnt them. It was three years afore she stopped writing. I feel quite sorry for her in a way. She just wanted better than round here.' She looked out at the street. 'Let's face it, I encouraged mine to find better and so did you. Not her though – Mrs Potter was having none of it. Selfish bitch.'

Sally stood up, putting on her coat and collecting her bag. She walked to the counter to pay the remains of her bill before leaving the coffee house.

With tears running down her face she went out into the rain, heading for the station. Under her breath she said, 'So the old bat didn't want me then. I should have come back sooner, or better still, never left. He is the only guy I loved and ever wanted.' Arriving at the train station, she sat on the waiting train, dreaming of what could have been.

An Old Photo Frame

It's unusual for me to go round car boot sales – I kind of think they just replaced jumble sales, a much needed staple of my childhood years. They were very useful for parents on a very small income, as many were back then. The school jumble sales were really good, as they leafletted the 'posh' areas, then collected on a given day, giving the clothes to volunteers at the school to sort into various lots, such as ladies', children's and men's clothing. On the day, queues would be enormous, snaking round the side of the school. Lots of people went in their winter coats, carrying a multitude of bags to put their bargains in.

In the school hall, trestle tables were positioned round the perimeter, leaving enough space for volunteers to work behind them. There was always a tea urn set up at the bottom of the hall, serviced by ladies wearing various scarves tied turban-like round their heads. Most of the ladies had colourful wrap over aprons and chattered 20 to the dozen. Their cups and saucers lined up a dozen across, five deep and three high, with enormous teapots that their slender arms did not seem to be able to manage. I do not recall coffee being available, though the school canteen and various supporters made fairy cakes. They call them muffins now-a-days.

Half a dozen formica tables that were easily cleaned, from the school canteen were set out; then silence fell as the headmaster's voice echoed round the hall. 'Two minutes ladies, it is going to be a hard first hour. Just do your best and thank you all for giving your time.'

The silence was profound, all listening intently, so quiet they could all hear the bolts being drawn back on the double doors as the caretaker shouted, 'Steady ladies!' There was no space in the corridor as the ladies raced for 'first pickings'. The hall was pandemonium for the next hour. Everything was two pence, regardless of what it was. From children's underwear to coats and shoes, men's shirts without collars, vests that would see this winter out, ladies' hand knitted cardigans, some to be unravelled to make something else, dresses and coats, although not many ladies' shoes. There were one or two well darned utility blankets that were later seen over a coat not quite warm enough to stay warm throughout the bleak winter.

Unwanted kitchen utensils, with a few pans and buckets with metal washers screwed in to stop the leaks. As crazy as it all was, it clothed all too many children whose parents could not afford shop prices. It also put money in the school funds that allowed the school to buy things they would not be able to afford and to give a quiet helping hand to the poorest of families in the school.

Car boots these days seem to be a mix of possible antiques and new goods including clothes, hardware items such as spanners and cleaning products at a cheaper rate than in the shops. I had come with a friend who simply wanted company. As she bargained at an 'antiques' stall I noticed, under other items, a picture frame. I carefully lifted it out, took a tissue out of my bag and gave it a once-over. It appeared to be tarnished silver that would shine up with a bit of silver polish. More interestingly, I liked the picture inside the frame.

No more than six inches by three, it was obviously very old and treasured, a typical photo of the time, probably taken with an old Box Brownie. The yellowing photo was of two children about five and seven years of age, sitting on a scrubbed white doorstep looking into the camera. The door, minus some of its paint, was wide open, allowing you to look into the hall, which appeared to only have its floorboards without any covering, though these also looked scrubbed clean. On the wall hung coat hooks, though I could only make out a cardigan or two.

My friend had finished her purchase, so I asked how much my frame would be. The stall holder, a woman of middle years, frizzy hair and broken mauve fingernails took the frame out of my hand, turned it over to reveal a broken back, then said, 'Pound.'

'You're joking,' said my friend, '50 pence is too much.'

'50 pence,' came the reply, as she placed it back on the stall, turning to serve another customer. I had 50 pence in my pocket, so handed it to her, retrieving the frame to put in my bag.

We finished our morning with coffee and bacon rolls, watching the market gradually come to a halt, listening to car boots closing till the following week. Some of the owners sat in the front of their cars counting their takings, shouting to each other 'good day' or 'best do better next week else I won't bother.'

When we had finished our rolls, Patricia, my friend, asked 'Why did you buy a picture frame, and a broken one at that?'

I looked into her sparking pale blue eyes, at her pale skin and almost white hair. So close to being an albino, though not quite. Patricia needed to cover her skin with a wide hat and long loose clothing, which seemed to suit her because of her height. Her voice is soft most of the time, but can be hard and determined when making a bargain or if there is something wrong. She held my eyes while continuing to sip the remains of her coffee.

'It was the picture, I replied, 'look' I reach into my bag bringing the picture out and onto the table. 'How often do you see this much history in a picture. It's black and white.' Pointing with a finger I said. 'Look at the faces of the children. Fed but not overfed, they're as thin as rakes. Look, look at his pudding bowl hair cut, so roughly cut, probably by his mother while dad was at work.' I smiled at the picture then at Patricia. 'Don't you just love those braces on his shoulders; look at the way they hang loose down the front.' I smiled. 'His trousers look like hand-me-downs and those crinkled socks round his shoes with his toes peeking out of both shoes and socks!' I took a closer look at the photo. 'As for the little girl?' I paused for a moment. 'Gosh, doesn't your heart go out to her. Her hair is pulled back into bunches.' I peer more closely at her. 'Look, they seem to be tied with old rags. Her dress has to be two sizes too big and covered with a pinny.'

I smiled to myself. 'I just love the photo. I'll try to get it copied, then probably buy a new frame too.'

Patricia shook her head with a smile. 'You always amaze me by picking up the strangest of things.'

I arrived home to find my husband, Stan, had walked through the house, leaving mud from front to back. Though I am not especially house-proud, I loathe him walking mud through from the allotment. The allotment was his only vice, and I have to admit the vegetables and flowers he brings home are worth a little bit of mud. If I had been home, he could have come in the back way, so I blamed myself partly for the mud.

As we greeted each other I noticed the smell of freshly dug vegetables filling the air. Stan said, 'I put the flowers in a bucket love, I know you will sort them yourself later.' He sniffed the air. 'The meat you left in smells about done, can I help with the vegetables?' he asked, standing in his old gardening socks on the cold tiled floor whilst holding his freshly washed wellingtons in his left hand.

'No Stan, it looks like you've done enough for one day. I'll put the kettle on and make you a cup of tea. Why don't you make yourself comfortable? I'll have dinner ready in half an hour.'

I love washing the fresh vegetables, and dinner was ready in half an hour. It was such a lovely evening we ate it in the garden, using the old, much-loved garden furniture that Stan made years ago. We washed up together, then Stan took a beer outside and I took a small glass of gin and tonic, and that is where we sat exchanging pleasantries, talking over our different days as long-married couples do.

Before going to the shops on the Monday, I put the picture in its frame in my bag. I really didn't have any shopping as such, so looked for a photo shop who would copy the picture and possibly improve it.

'Could I have it slightly enlarged?'

The slim young man in the shop was used to people updating photos. 'No problem.' The finished picture would be ready on Friday. I chose a new frame while I was in the shop, agreeing to pick up the photo in its new frame Friday morning.

Arriving back home, I found Stan just putting down the phone. 'Hi love,' he said. 'I've just been speaking to Cousin Sue. She has to go away for a week and wondered if we would have her mother to stay to help her out. I said yes. The old dear was no trouble last time she was here. Have I done right?'

'Course you have. I keep the room ready so it will be no bother. I love her staying – she takes up no time and is such fun to be with. When is she coming?'

'Friday evening, then staying over to the following Sunday.' A pause as he went into the kitchen to put the kettle on. 'They said all she has in the evening is her cocoa and a biscuit, so not to worry about dinner for them.'

Sue and her husband Reg arrived around seven, staying long enough to explain about her mother's pills. We would not have any problems as the chemist sorts them all out for her. All we need to do is to make sure she takes the right ones at the right time. Then they were gone, and poor old Aunt Sarah was still in the hall wearing her brown coat with a feathered hat on her head, looking rather bemused standing by her old battered cardboard case.

Stan and I helped her out of her coat and hat asking if she would like a drink. Her rheumy, light grey eyes gazed at us. With a mischievous grin she asked for 'a large G & T. It is a nice evening so could we please drink it sitting in the garden?' That is what we did.

The following morning Sarah came into the kitchen holding the newly framed picture, which I had put on the night cupboard by her bed, in her curled hand. She carefully sat at the table, placing the picture so gently by her plate. She looked up with wet eyes. 'How ever did you manage to find this?' she said in a tearful voice.

'At a car boot sale last Sunday.' I sat holding her hand. 'Do you know them?' I asked.

She dabbed her eyes with a lovely white embroidered handkerchief. Sniffed a couple of times then looked at me. 'So do you.'

'I don't think so, how could I know these two children?' I asked. She laughed quietly as Stan came to the table.

'Stan, do you recognise these children?' Stan looked at Aunt Sarah, then, gently taking the picture from her hand, looked more closely at it. 'Have to say they look familiar,' he said, 'but I really don't know why.'

Sarah chuckled. 'I was about five when this was taken.' She smiled at the photo. 'Taken at our nan's it was. We had been left there as mum was in the hospital and dad had to work. Nan agreed to take us in till mum was well.'

'What was wrong with her?' I asked

'No idea, they didn't tell kiddies in those days.'

'Is that boy my dad?' asked an astounded Stan.

'Right, he is your dad – quite mischievous as well. I guess we both were. I remember the time we decided to go scrumping in May.'

'In May?' Stan and I said in unison.

'Yes, in May! Some older children told us where to go. Well, you see,' she looked at us, her eyes sparkling, 'we were a couple of townies, just houses and back yards where we came from, not even a local park. We played in the street unless there were trouble, then it was the small paved back yard with the lavi in the far corner.' Looking back at the photo, she continued, 'We took one of Nan's bags, hoping to help her by scrumping some apples. We peered round the fence in the wall and were mesmerised. We slowly went into the orchard to see all these trees in flower, dragging Nan's bag behind us. We stood gaping up at the flowers and the bees going from flower to flower. It was a wonderful sight.' She paused, her eyes in a distant memory we could not see, smiling as she and her brother stood mesmerised.

'We didn't even jump when a voice asked gruffly, 'What you two doing here?' We just stood looking upwards at the trees. Your dad answered after a minute or two.

'Oh mister, it is so very pretty.'

I chimed in 'How do they get so pretty?' I kept turning round, so slowly, 'What are all those bees doing?'

We finally looked at the man questioningly. He was not very tall, dressed in navy overalls and a shirt without a collar, his flat cap in his hand scratching his head as he looked at us.

'Where you two from then?'

Tom answered, 'We're with Nan while mum's ill. The trees sir, some big boys told us we could get apples. We thought it would help out Nan, but there are no apples, but they look really pretty, don't they?'

He stared at us then told us gently 'You don't get apples till October time. Now is when the bees pollinate the flowers so that apples grow.'

We both looked back up at the trees with big 'O's' on our faces. He was a kindly man, going into his shed to bring out two large apples for nan. His wife, who had stood silently with amusement in her eyes, gave us a glass of lemonade each.

They said to go home to Nan, and if we were still there in October, we could collect a bag of windfalls for her. He smiled as he took us back out the gate.'

Shrugging her shoulders with a sigh, she said, 'We didn't know. We tried to ignore the older boys after that, but it was a magical couple of hours.' Aunt Sarah continued eating breakfast with her memories.

Sitting in the garden in the shade after breakfast, Aunt Sarah was lost in the photo and the memories it held for her. Finally, as Stan brought out her morning tea and biscuits, she said 'There was the time Tom and me decided to catch some fish for our tea. We heard some lads talking saying that the dew pond was teaming this year... We trailed to the field and there was a pond. We climbed over the gate, taking our sticks with string dangling from the end. We dangled them into the water, taking care not to get our shoes too muddy. How long we stood there I have no idea. Our concentration was such we had not heard a tractor stop outside the gate.

'What the hell?' We looked up, frightened, but the burly man looked scared. In his green muddy wellingtons, he grabbed the pair of us, throwing us both over the hedge onto a trailer bed. Shaking, we both stood up to see a herd of cows racing to the gate.

'It's bloody milking time, you idiots.'

We watched frozen in place, arms round each other as we watched the cattle trundling though the gate and ahead of the tractor. Eventually, when the gate was closed on the empty field the man came back to us having retrieved Nan's trampled bag. He looked up at our frightened faces. 'You two staying with Nanny Higgins?' We looked at each other, then nodded. 'Why did you come here?' Silence. 'Why did you think you could come here?' We both burst into tears. 'Who told you to come? Look, you're both safe. Sit down and I'll take you to your Nan's'.

So we went back on a tractor trailer to see both Nan and Grandad looking up and down the street looking worried. They both took us off the trailer and Nan took us inside, while Grandad spoke at length with the man. Our faces mopped, with a biscuit and a small glass of milk, we sat in the garden till we stopped shaking. After tea we were told quite firmly not to listen to lads and stay away from the fields unless Grandad was with us.'

'Did you see the tractor driver again?'

'Yes, many times. He always gave us a wave and a big smile. I think I need to have my nap now.'

With her arm on Stan's he walked her into her ground floor bedroom, helped to take her shoes off and closed the curtain.

This set the tone for the week, Aunt Sarah with the frame in her hand regaling us both about the mischievous things the pair of them got up to, keeping us all laughing.

When Sue came on Sunday, Sarah showed her the photo. Sue didn't know the little girl was her mother, so was delighted at the rare photo of her mother growing up. 'Why don't you take it with you,' I said. 'It really belongs to you.' Sarah smiled her thanks.

Six months later, Sarah had a fall, causing her to go into hospital where her health declined, dying four weeks later. After her funeral Sue gave us a package to take home with us. Later, at home, with his nightly glass of beer, Stan opened up the package, which contained the photo of his dad and Aunty Sarah with a letter reading, 'Thank you for letting me take the photo home. It held so many happy memories. I hope it will for you too. Love Aunty Sarah.'

We both smiled at the photo frame, then giggled at the tales we had been told.

A Misunderstanding

Sonia and Peter had been at loggerheads every time they met up. Well, not every time, but it certainly seemed like it. They had even begun to sleep in separate bedrooms! Sonia cried herself to sleep most nights wondering what had gone wrong. They had always been so good together, but Peter had become so very secretive.

Fortunately, Peter went out earlier in the mornings than she did, so her door remained closed till she heard him drive away. She tidied her room after showering and dressed so she was ready to go down to the kitchen to have a quick breakfast before collecting her red bicycle to go to work.

Arriving in the kitchen, she noticed Peter's breakfast things on the side. 'I am not clearing up after you!' she shouted bitterly. Collecting her own breakfast, she sat glaring at Peter's plates. 'No, this has gone on for long enough. It is time I did something,' she said to his dirty dishes, washed up her used dishes and tidied them away, leaving Peter's dishes where he had left them.

Putting on her light grey coat with pink trim and picking up her phone, handbag and keys, she left the house in a huff. Her bicycle was in the lean-to, she walked it past the newly paved car port, out the gate onto the road, before sitting on her saddle, putting her bag and phone in a pink side-pannier, and off she went to work.

During the day her concerned colleagues watched as she worried her bottom lip from time to time. She would normally join in the teasing at break time, but not today. She was too distracted to pay attention to anything for long, so unlike her. Come lunch time she realised she had not made herself a lunch so, ignoring her colleagues, she walked to the local coffee house for a coffee and a sandwich sitting on her own in a corner. Slowly, without enthusiasm, she took sips of her tasteless coffee. When she left the coffee house she also left behind the untouched sandwich and half a cup of coffee.

On her way back to work she called into a lettings agency to find out how much a small flat would cost, taking to work a list of properties currently available.

Sonia phoned a couple of landlords. Instead of going straight home after work, she looked at two possible flats, finding out what she would get for what she could afford. Not very much, she thought, but she could not live in the atmosphere at home. Not wanting to go home, Sonia decided to go down to the beach, where she bought a portion of chips and mushy peas from a restaurant, taking them to the top of the shingle where she sat to pick at them, throwing most of the chips to the hungry seagulls.

Lifting up her red bicycle from the stones, she walked along the costal path aimlessly, muttering from time to time 'What am I going to do?' Reaching the next coastal town, Sonia decided to take a seat o the green-sward in front of the blue and yellow beach huts to gather her thoughts. She chose a bench where she could look at the huts, remembering as a child begging her parents to buy one. Now she just smiled at the childish thought. No more than a shed with a makeshift shelf to put a Bunsen burner on. No toilet. No water. 'What a silly child I was', she said to the blue beach hut just in front of her. She paused, and said 'No, not a silly child, I just didn't know you couldn't live in them, and that was what I thought I could do and wanted then.'

As the moon rose to follow the sun in the sky, she stood up dejectedly, turning her bike homewards. She cycled slowly, still pondering what to do about the awkward situation with Peter. 'Do I stay, or do I go and start again?' Childhood was so simple in comparison, being a grown up is not very easy, though all teenagers think it is. 'Do I throw away ten years or stop and sort it out? Where did it all go wrong?' She stopped by the kerb. 'What happened to change everything?'

Peter becoming very secretive was where it all started. He went from sharing most evenings together to being mostly on his own often out of the house for long periods. On the days Peter was in, he swallowed his meal before going into his study to read. However, when she tapped on the door with a drink, he would throw things into drawers, locking them. What did he need to hide? Sonia had looked round the study when she cleaned, but only came in contact with locked drawers, why? 'Neither of us ever locked anything until now. How long ago was that? Must be at least three months.' Yes, at least three months ago, it was just after Sally's birthday.

'Have you found someone else?' she asked. He just smiled and told her to stop worrying. How could she stop worrying, when he had not previously excluded her? There were the phone calls that went dead if she answered. Sonia mentioned it to Peter a number of times, wondering if they should contact their provider. Peter's reply was 'Stop being oversensitive.' Sonia started to sob, she could not help it. There had to be another person involved. Here she was, sitting on her red cycle in her work clothes, sobbing in the street.

A number of people walked past. A kindly lady with white hair and blue eyes put a hand on her arm. 'My dear, it probably is not as bad as you think it is. Will it help if I listen to you? A problem shared is often a problem halved, you know, especially between strangers.'

Sonia dried her eyes, found a smile and thanked her for caring. The lady told her to go home, as she felt things would be different when she arrived there. 'You will wonder then why you wasted so much time in torment.' Sonia smiled and thanked her but did not believe her kind words.

Not having eaten properly all day and now feeling a little lightheaded Sonia walked the rest of the way home. Not use to being out so late on her own for years she enjoyed the quietness of the streets in the dusk. Windows being lit as lights were slowly going on in the houses. Sonia was surprised that all the lights were on in her house. The oak stained front door was open, Sonia could see people in the house, all seemingly busy.

A nice little pink two-seater car was parked where Peter usually parked his car. Her heart sank as did her shoulders. It is true then. He has found another person. How long would it be before she had to move out? Sighing deeply with a shudder Sonia put her bike away. 'I do not see why, as the injured party, I should leave the house,' she told the bike as she turned to go into her home.

As she walked through the door, Peter came into the hall from the kitchen. He stopped and stared at her. His face as white as chalk. 'What has happened?' Sonia asked.

'Sonia, Sonia,' he shouted, rushing towards her, engulfing her in his arms. He sobbed into her dark hair, then into her neck. 'Sonia, my Sonia, where have you been?'

Her sister came out of the lounge. 'Where have you been, what do you think you are playing at causing all this upset?' She shouted loud enough for the whole street to hear.

Sonia was stunned. 'What upset and what does it have to do with you anyway?'

Jane gawked at her before replying, 'We have been on to the police to report you as a missing person, that is what it has to do with me.' She pulled herself up to her full height of five and a half feet, daring Sonia to argue further.

Peter pulled himself apart slightly with tears still running down his face looked into her own pale face. He realised she was shaking. 'Sonia why are you shaking so?' He asked wiping a hand over his own wet face. 'Have you eaten today? Your lunch is still in the fridge?' Sonia was too emotional to speak so just shook her head.

He took her into the lounge helping to remove her coat. On a sob he said 'Just sit there, I have made dinner it is still hot, I will bring you some on a plate.'

'Wants a good talking to,' said Jane, taking the chair opposite Sonia then looked concern as in the clear electric light she looked into her strained white face, her dark hair, usually so tidy in a mess blown by the sea breezes, her eyes swollen and red. Sonia sobbed deeply, though without tears. I think I had cried out all my tears.

Peter brought in a small plate of my favourite dish, a lamb goulash. It smelt lovely. He spooned some into her mouth then went back to the kitchen to get me a glass of water. When she had finished, he took the plate and glass away, then took her hands in his. 'Sonia what has got into you this last few months?' She snatched her hands away. 'What has got into me?' I shouted. 'How about what has got into you these last few months?'

'I don't understand,' he paused, 'what do you mean?' he asked, taken back.

'You don't understand?' Sonia stood up on shaky legs. 'You don't understand about hiding away in the study, throwing everything into drawers if I entered it?' My slim chest heaved with a wheeze. I pointed my hand stabbing it in his chest. 'You don't understand about the phone calls that go dead if I answered them? When do we spend time together?' I paused. 'Never. Not these last few months.' I stumbled round the room, my shoulders hunched, looking back at him. 'You... You spend all your spare time in your study with locked drawers.' My chest wheezed again as I took another deep breath. 'I... I moved out of our bedroom and you did nothing. Nothing! You said nothing. You don't care. What kind of husband does not ask 'WHY?' when his wife leaves his bed? I ask you if you found someone else and you just smirk.' The room went silent in anticipation of a bigger climax.

He looked into my ravaged face. 'Sonia, Sonia, I am so very sorry. I... I did not realise that I was hurting you so badly.'

'I... I did ask if you found someone else, but you just walked away with a smirk. What do you expect me to think?' I shouted at him.

Only her broken sobs filled the room. Peter stood up slowly as realisation of the situation dawned on him. He did not realise the length of his secrecy or the toll it had on Sonia. Maybe, just maybe, he taken the secrecy too far! Taking her left hand, he led her out of their front door to the side of the lovely, pink two-seater car. Out of his pocket he took some keys. He took her right hand, putting the keys in it. She looked at him bemused.

'Darling Sonia, tomorrow is our tenth anniversary. You have gone without so much so we could get the house...' He checked his own voice. 'I… I wanted to do something special for you. I really don't like you cycling to work, especially in the winter, so I thought you would like this car to go to work and go about town in? Am I wrong?' he asked quietly.

He turned her gently towards him. Looking down at her with his clear blue eyes, taking in her ravaged face, he asked, 'Can you forgive me if I promise not to do anything like this again? I love you so much and yes, we will spend more time together. I promise you there is not anyone else, nor will there ever be, you are all I need. I love you so much.'

Sonia looked at the keys, at the car and into his worried eyes.

'This,' she looked at the car, 'this is all for me?' She gasped on a sob.

'I have been longing to tell you, I was promoted at work and received a small bonus, which I wanted to spend on you, and this is what I thought you needed most.'

She fell into his strong comforting arms sobbing, 'Thank you, thank you.'

'Does this mean we will share the same bedroom again?' Peter asked gently with a smile.

Sonia nodded into his wet shirt.

They went back inside the house to see Jane with tears in her eyes. Jane hugged her sister, then Peter, before she left them, taking her husband with her while shaking her head, bemused. Various neighbours also left, closing the front door behind them.

Peter and Sonia walked into the kitchen-diner, where a table had been set complete with wine for two people and candles. This is where they sat till late talking about his promotion, the bonus, but mostly enjoying each other's company once again.

The Shed

I had come home to find that the kitchen door was open. I was
sure I had closed it. Puzzled, I listened to the house; nothing
seemed different. The silence pounded on my ears, while the
cold draught from the door wafted round my legs. Shrugging
my shoulders, I closed the door before continuing through into
the kitchen, glancing round to find the dining table festooned
with tinsel and baubles. Centred on the table sat a medium-sized,
square brown box. The house was still silent apart from the gur-
gling of the heating system. Removing my outdoor clothes while
keeping my eye on the brown box, I noticed a white card writ-
ten in a childish hand.

'For you,' it said. I made my drink, then pulled out a chair at
the table. 'How did it get here?' I thought, 'You can't get in here
from the garden. I've been out all day. No-one would call.' As my
sad day drifted away, I started to ask, 'The decorations...where
did they come from?' I paced wearily round the kitchen, intently listening. No strange sounds. The hum of the boiler zipping
in and out. The creak of boards where pipes lay. No. Nothing.
Having finished my coffee, I gently lifted the box.

'Is it empty?' I lifted it to my ear. Not a sound when I rat-
tle it. 'This is a sick joke.' I took the box to the rubbish bin outside the back door, replacing the lid rather clumsily. In its echo
I returned to the table, gathering all the tinsel carefully rolling
it all into separate colours. The baubles. 'What am I going to do
with them? They can all go to a charity shop! I am in no mood
for Christmas.'

I tap the table gently. 'The box, I can put them all in the
box.' Returning to the bin I recovered the box. It is well taped.

'Good, it will hold all this rubbish.' I slit the box with a knife, then dumped the knife in the sink. Lifting the lid, I started to place the baubles in the box, before noticing a piece of paper was stuck to the bottom of the box. 'I am so sorry for the trouble I caused you. Can you forgive me?' I slipped on to a chair. 'Who am I supposed to forgive?' In smaller letters I read, 'gift in shed'. Gift in shed. The large computer print gave nothing away.

'Gosh! No-one has used that shed since she left. No! It couldn't be! Could it?' I grabbed the shed key and a torch, throwing the back door to bang against the wall. I ran to the shed lying in the darkness. I fumbled with the key. My hands felt for the light switch. Brightness illuminated the dusty shed, though it was as I remembered it. Her den.

A small child of about four years gets out of her chair, holding a kitten out towards me. 'We thought you would like a kitten, only we didn't want her to be shut in a box.' We walk towards each other as she offers the kitten out to me.

I kneel down in front of her. 'Who are you?' I ask, looking into familiar eyes.

'I need a granny and Mummy thought you might like to be my granny.'

'Sorry Mum, I have missed you so much. Can we stay?' came my daughter's voice from behind me. The past arguments evaporated. I stood turning, as the tears rolled down my face. My arms are open. She stepped into them with her own tears.

We stood together till an impatient voice exclaimed, 'Mum the kitten needs feeding and I'm hungry! When can we eat?'

We both laugh. 'You had better come to the house then. We can order a takeaway for tonight. What do you prefer, Indian or Chinese?'

I Closed the Door

I close the door behind me. It should be a small task, closing the door. Somehow, over the years, it has become difficult because of my acquired pettiness. The door must be closed silently. Why? I do not know. However, I close the door quietly on the debris behind it. I can sort it another day.

Walking to the kitchen-diner, I make my forbidden coffee. Why is it that everyone thinks coffee is bad for you? Drinking coffee by the bucket-load, they lecture me on my small daily coffee. Carers they call themselves. Wouldn't know what caring is. Hmm. My small indulgence isn't significant in the grand scheme of things. Gratefully, I sit at the hard wood table with my latte. I've become good at making it over the year, coffee that is. Just the right amount of coffee granules, thick black simmered with cardamom and milk. Luxury! Not that coffee house rubbish. My mind floats back to the debris behind the door as I lift my mug to drink.

How did it all get there? More importantly, how did it become such a mess?

I have been complaining for months about hearing noises. They, the carers, keep telling me it was all in my mind. Well, there is nothing wrong with my mind. I leave my half-finished coffee, choosing to go back to the room now.

I gently open the door to look round the room. The occasional tables, so loved, have been turned over. One lying flat upside down, another looking as though it had been used as a wheel. My precious memories. My ornaments brought back from far-flung places were scattered across the carpet from wall to wall. Walking slowly towards them, I kneel on the floor to gently gather them back to the upside down table.

Each one is a treasured memory left for me by my husband. He was one for gathering ornaments on our travels. The china ladies were his favourites. We laughed together. I told him he would need to collect them in every pose, though I had no idea he would like nude ladies. Smiling at the thought, I sigh. Men will be men, I guess. My choice was pretty boxes, though mostly in the same style. Round with fitting lids, all decorated with exotic flowers. I gathered up the Lady from Greece. Sitting back on my heels, I hold her gently. It was our first. Not the best example, but we were young and just wanted something. Something to remind us of our first holiday abroad.

Walking on my knees to the upside-down table, placing her gently on it, I notice the new chip on her. I return to gather up other ladies and trinket boxes, some now with broken lids. Oh dear. What a waste. I pile up the magazines in neat piles as much as I can, though these remain on the carpet, a floral affair white with bunches of spring flowers, a warm contrast to the plain white walls. Using an overturned chair as an aid, I carefully lift myself to standing looking round the floor to see if there was something else I could put right. What time will the cleaners come this week? They are not as reliable as they were when Steve was here with me. They all liked him, his easy way and quick smile. How I miss him.

Hearing a noise, I pause to listen. Was that the front door? I turn towards the door to listen. Who is that? Why are they here? It is Thursday today; I usually have visitors on Friday or Sunday and Mondays. Why would someone come today?

'There had been a burglary,' a deep voice was speaking, 'though there is no sign of a break-in.'

'Do you think the old gal knew who it was then?'

'No idea, though best to be a bit more respectful. By all accounts she was a very popular old lady. Best refer to her by name, or lady at least.'

'OK Sir, the old lady, what was her name?'

'Mantel, Mrs Maud Mantel. She and her late husband did a lot of good in the area. Highly respected couple.'

Mantel, Maud Mantel, that is me, I am Maud Mantel! Who are they? I press my ear against the door listening intently as two heavy treads went up the stairs. The sound of hob-nailed boots walking across the boards above my head.

'Nothing seems disturbed much in here Sir?' comes the younger voice.

'We don't think whoever damaged the front room came any further into the house.'

'Strange that, sir. You'd have thought they would have gone all the way through the house.'

'Wouldn't have done them any good. They were not a rich couple, though there is talk they were loaded. How they were loaded we don't know. Got people working on it.'

'Why only the lounge?'

A single pair of boots walks into another bedroom. They walk round the room. I can hear draws being opened and closed. They are wasting their time. Nothing was ever kept in that room much. It was a guest bedroom.

A guest bedroom. Why did we wish to have a guest bedroom? Few people visited us, let alone stayed here. I remember the luxury linen I bought for guests. The careful planning of the floor, should it be carpet or a nice wooden floor? Curtains should be blackout, as the room faced east catching the sunrise. Wardrobe with matching drawers and soft furnishings. They were fun to buy, a springtime theme. I wanted to put a sign up saying 'Springtime', but Steve said no. We were never in to have visitors, always out, doing good. I lean gently on the door jamb. Too busy to entertain in our own home. The boots leave the guest bedroom returning to my bedroom.

'Sir! Is it possible that one of the care workers let someone in?'

'Why let someone in when you have access anyway?'

'Well Sir, perhaps the old lady, Mrs Maud Mantel, spent all her day in the lounge. The only way they could search the lounge was when she was asleep.'

'Hmm.' Silence. 'I guess that's plausible, but why wreck the room? What was in that room someone thought was important enough to do that much damage?' Silence again.

'Was there something in their past?'

'You find 'the something', and I'll let you follow it up.'

Two pairs of boots come echoing down the stairs coming towards me. The door opens and two police officers walk past me to look round the room. More cupboards and drawers were opened, though in all honesty, most of the contents were on the floor.

The younger officer has fair hair with brown eyes. How I had longed for a child, but it did not happen for us. I watch, fascinated, as they trawl through the debris. This young officer stands the tables upright, replacing some of the ornaments onto them.

'When will her funeral be, Sir?'

'No idea, we are trying to trace any relatives.'

'Did the burglar kill her?'

'No. Sadly died in her sleep. Guess when he realised she was dead he fled.'

'Me, dead? I am dead! Why am I still here if I am dead?'

I follow the officers from the room into the hall. They open the front door then both pause looking back on the room. I walk through the door and down the path, pausing at the open gate. I turn round to watch the pair. The younger man closes the door quietly behind him. Looking back at the road I laugh – I am free to run at last, so I do, up the hill towards the park.

That Ring!

I love watching the movement of the waves on a warm summer day, especially when the incoming tide sweeps the herrings in towards the waiting herring gulls, standing majestically with eyes only for the sea, patiently judging the sea and distance before taking to the sky to dive for their lunch, bringing their catch back to shore to eat.

A child I had seen frequently came running, calling out for his mother to hurry up. From their accents, they were Australian. She was willowy, with fair skin and fair hair that floated from under her large hat in the light breeze.

Today her son stopped to sit alongside me on the bench. His brown eyes looked shyly at me. I was surprised; he looked like my own lost boy Brian. Looking at me he asked, 'Do I know you?'

I replied, 'Probably not. You're Australian. I'm English.' He sat, thoughtful, for a few seconds before dashing off on tanned legs to join his mother.

Gathering my thoughts as I walked through the Arcade to Costa's for a bacon sandwich and a coffee, I mused about the little boy with brown eyes who looked so like my own son. His walk was so familiar as his impulsiveness.

I was an unmarried mother, giving birth to a lovely boy I named Brian, while his father went off to wherever worthless men go. I worked hard to bring him up, going to evening classes while a kind neighbour kept an eye out for me. I used to do the same for her, though she usually went to the pub. By the time Brian started school I had earned five 'O' levels and two 'A's. Feeling more confident, I went looking for work.

I sipped my coffee, reminding myself I was lucky, working through an agency for a small company who helped me with time off with Brian. We were happy together, Brian and I, enjoying each other's company. I smile at his early years, the Christmases we had with a cardboard cut-out tree we decorated with hand-made decorations.

The school years and the friends we had round our table to enjoy a meal, then a trip to the park for a ball game, as well as time to play on the equipment there. Lovely memories.

Brian went to university learning to be an engineer. Though living away, he came back regularly so we could still spend some time together, bringing a friend or two. He finally graduated, returning to a position with an engineering company, close enough to live at home. It was a happy, peaceful existence... till he brought her home.

I tried to get along, but she, Ruth, was so full of criticism. I felt like I could do nothing right, for Brian, madam and eventually for myself. After about eighteen months I came home from work early with a migraine to find her in my bedroom going through my possessions. She had several rings of mine on her hands. 'What are you doing in here? Take those rings off,' I said quite crossly.

'I can do what I like. Brian will believe me, and this house will be mine.'

'What?' My shoulders shook, my headache became blinding. 'What do you mean, this house will be yours?'

'Brian believes everything I say. You will not stand a chance. You!' She pointed her ringed fingers at me, 'You will be out on the streets. This house will be mine.'

I stumbled to the bed. 'I am unwell, I'm not thinking straight.' My glazed eyes looked at her leering face. 'Get out, get out and leave those rings in here.' She flung the rings across the room looking down at me with scorn and anger.

'I will take Brian from you unless you are really good to me.' She bent to look into my face. 'Just remember that.' She left the room, slamming the door so hard it echoed through the house and my painful head for several minutes. I undressed and fell into bed after swallowing some migraine relief tablets from the bathroom cabinet.

I remained in bed for several days, then stumbled round the house avoiding Ruth, who made no effort to do as much as wash up a cup. Brian was silent when he came home from work each evening.

Then came that fateful evening. 'Mum, I know there has only been us two. It can be difficult when another comes in the house to live.' He paused, looking into my eyes to make sure I was listening. 'Ruth grew up in care, it is hard for her to have a family. You could help more round the house.' He looked at me, then cautiously added, 'Perhaps you could help her some more?'

'Doing what?' I asked guardedly.

'Cleaning, shopping and cooking.'

'Cleaning what?' I asked louder. 'What has that lazy bitch cleaned?'

'Mum', please don't talk about Ruth like that.' Though he was clearly shaken he remained calm.

'What has she ever cooked?' I glared at him, anger moving quickly to the surface. Pointing at myself, 'I cook when I come home from work. I wash up her breakfast dishes and her lunch mess.'

'Mum,'

'No Brian, it will not do.' Shaking my head, I continue, 'I work all day, I come home each night to clean up the mess created while I am out. I,' pointing at myself, 'I buy the food, I cook the food.' I look at him getting really angry. 'I', pointing at me, 'I clean the kitchen again.' Shaking now with temper unleashed, 'Please do tell me what that paragon of virtue does all day. I want to know what she cooks, what she cleans and where she buys the bloody groceries.'

'I give her money for the housekeeping, I…'

'Where is it then, because I am spending all my money keeping the pair of you. I have not had any money for myself since she came into this house.' I stand upright, rigid. 'Well, where is the money? I cannot keep feeding the pair of you on my earnings.'

'That's it, Mum!' Brian is now as angry as I am. 'Ruth is a good person, and you are jealous. I'll find somewhere to stay so you will not be able to be so cruel to my future wife.'

'Wife. Wife. Marrying her will be the worst thing you will do. She is no good to anyone.'

'That's it, we will be out of here as quickly as we can.' He turned walking out of the kitchen slamming the door behind him. I slumped back at the table with my head in my hands. 'What have I done? What have I done?'

They moved out on the Friday while I was at work, taking three of my rings! True, I didn't wear them often, but they were my rings. Two were from my parents for birthday presents. The other, three large diamonds set in gold, Brian's dad had given me, inscribed 'you are my only one'. How could my son change so much he would steal my treasured rings? I sighed.

I haven't heard from Brian since then, fourteen years ago. I heard they had left their lodgings. The child running on the prom reminded me of Brian. The way he moved his hands. The way he held his head. The way his hair fell over his left eye. My world taken by that lazy selfish bitch!

I stood up to leave. 'Still, life is good,' I told myself. 'I left the past behind, moving to a new area, a new job and new friends. Just focus on the present.'

A few days later I walked back to the same seat on the prom with a coffee to wait for Janice, a friend, to join me. We both have a day off planning to go to lunch and visit the shops. The Australian child returned with his mother. He looked at me and asked if I was his grandmother. I laughed gently. 'Probably not, though I think I would like to be.'

His mother spoke in a strong Australian accent. 'He's missing his dad. He normally works in Horsham but has had to go north for a week or two. He should be home tonight, then we intend to live here in Bognor.' She gave me a puzzled look, before taking an old ring box out of her bag.

'I think this might be yours.' She placed a box on my lap. I look at a rather old and tattered ring box. I look up at her questioningly.

I gently picked up the box noticing toddler's teeth marks on one side. I paused, stood up slowly, dropping my coffee to the promenade where it splashed towards the sea.

'Who are you?' I felt my shoulders stiffen. The raging anger I had not felt since moving here began to crawl up my spine and down through my body. I began to shake. 'What do you want?' I pause, shaking the box. 'Why are you giving me this?' I held the box up almost pushing it into her face. 'What game do you think you are playing?' The red mist was descending fast. 'How dare you...'

An arm pulled me away.

'Val, Val,' I was pulled away but could not see. 'Val, whatever is going on?' I finally recognised the voice of my friend Janice. I shake more violently. My head started to clear. I put the box on the seat. Janice picked up my bag looking questioningly at the Australian lady, who stood stunned and frightened, holding her son behind her.

'Come Val, my car is just a little way up the road.' She half supported and half dragged me to her car and opened the door, pushing me into the passenger seat. We drove off after Janice had put my seat belt on me.

I came to my senses after we had been sat for a while in a quiet corner in The Bishop's garden in Chichester. I was sat looking towards the fountain. Janice was beside me. 'Will you be OK while I go for a couple of drinks?' I nodded silently.

When Janice returned, we sat quietly for a while.

'Sorry Janice. Demons took over for a while.'

'Looked more than demons. They looked scared to death. What happened?'

'She gave me a red box.' I began to shake again. Janice took the coffee from my hand. My voice rose. 'The red box with teeth marks. He's dead.' I shouted standing up. 'She killed him.' I kicked the bench. 'She killed him; I know she killed him.' I hit a nearby tree then kicked ineffectually at a shrub. I fell to my knees shouting 'She killed him. She killed my precious boy.' The tears fell uncontrollably. I was out of it. I no longer knew that I was thumping the ground. I felt a pin prick. I passed out.

I woke in a hospital bed. It was early morning. A lady held my hand.

'You are in hospital Val. You are safe. Breakfast is soon. Try to eat and especially drink some water. A consultant will be seeing you later this morning. I'm Margery.' Margery, a similar age to me, wore jeans and a shirt top. She sat with me till breakfast. Helped me sit up. Pushed the tray towards me, lifting a beaker of water into my hand waiting till I had drained it all, refilled the beaker replacing it on the tray.

'Do you think you can manage to eat something?' I nodded dully at her. My tray held a plastic bowl containing cornflakes and milk, a plastic spoon, and the beaker refilled with water. Another beaker had weak sweetened tea; milk had also been added. I leaned back against the pillar. I looked round the room. Small, clinical, clean. The wide window draped with pink curtains, showed a view of woods and a garden. I sat back up – a patio door!

'The injection you had will wear off in another hour. I picked up the spoon and began to eat my breakfast. Margery smiled gently. 'I'll be back in about twenty minutes.' I smiled my thanks.

After the cornflakes and weak tea, I explored the room. Ensuite! Very nice; almost hotel standard. Then I walk back to the patio door. Surprisingly it opened easily onto a sunlit patio. This is where Margery found me.

'Here are your clothes, they're freshly washed. Get dressed and I'll show you to the morning room. Take a shower, I'll be back in twenty.' She put my clothes on a chair leaving hurriedly.

I looked into the mirror in the bathroom. I looked a mess. Sunken eyes in a white face, hair needing a brush. 'Come on girl, you can do better than this.' I showered, there was a brush on the shelf to tidy up my hair. I dressed hurriedly. I felt surprisingly better, though anxious, but that could be the residue of the injection. I had no idea where I was, but cheerful sounds come in through the closed door. I wandered to the patio door. I was not quite ready to mix with people yet.

A couple of plastic chairs and a plastic table were set on the patio, so I positioned one chair facing towards the woods but was out of the sun. I was there a long time, wondering how I had arrived at this lovely location. Why had I been given an injection? Slowly it all came back. The Australian woman and her ring box. I placed my hand over my mouth. I felt deep shame as the scene played back in my head. Tears rolled silently down my face.

'How could I treat a young mother so badly? Her little lad must have been so frightened. That bloody ring!' I said out loud. 'Why, oh why did I keep the bloody thing?' I sat still looking towards the woods but not seeing anything. 'I love him, that is why I still kept the ring, I just can't stop loving him. Why did he not stay in touch?'

I looked at the trees. A sly fox was crouched low to the ground. I focused on it as it curled up in the shade. I sighed deeply as a tray was placed on the table. I turned to see a man of similar age to Margery. He smiled widely his blue eyes twinkling.

'I thought you would like a large coffee.' He looked round as though seeing if anyone was watching. 'If anyone asks, it's water, OK?'

I smiled, then laughed at the absurdity of the situation. Coffee. Water. 'Thank you.'

'I am Doctor Michael, but everyone here calls me Michael. Sugar?' He looked at me with raised eyebrows.

'Yes please.'

'Right Val, is it ok to call you Val, or would you like to be Mrs. Stevens?'

'No, Val is fine. Where are we Michael, how did I get here?' I looked into the frothy coffee topped with cream and sprinkled with chocolate shavings.

'This is not the first time you have ended up in one of these units, though I think this time you will be back at work quickly.' He stirred several heaped spoonfuls of brown sugar into his coffee, which matched mine.

'You have been here four days; we sedated you to calm you down.' He took several gulps of his coffee. 'I want you to tell me about who gave you the ring and why he left.' He looked at my surprised face. 'Sorry, I have been standing just inside the door listening.'

I drank some of my coffee before gently replacing it on the table.

'I met Peter when I was nineteen.' I smiled at the memory. 'My parents did not like him, not for any reason other than he worked away from home a lot. He worked as an engineer on the oil rigs.' I sighed deeply. 'I fell in love with him as soon as we met. We complimented each other. He had fair hair to my dark hair.' I leaned on the table as a smile crept unasked for in my voice. 'We had similar interests; both of us liked just to walk, especially in parks and wooded areas. Sometimes he would drive to hillier areas so we could climb something without going too far from home.' I smiled at the memory of us racing down a hillside, both ending up losing our footing and rolling the rest of the way. We were oblivious of those round us.

'We had coffees in out of the way places.' I stroked my coffee cup while remembering us holding hands across a table. 'We ate in country pubs, only aware of each other and the scents around us. The smell of old leather mixed with the hop smell of beer and cigarettes. Lilac gardens with old apple trees holding rope swings.' I sighed. 'He asked me to move in with him. He had a two bedroom flat not far from where I lived. 'Yes,' I answered without thought. 'The next time I am home, in three months' time, we will be together for always. This is a ring I had made especially for you.' He handed me an expensive red ring box. Inside was a gold ring with three large diamonds. Inscribed inside were the words, 'You are my only one.'

'My parents were horrified! Move in with him without marriage first? No. 'If you do, you need not knock on this door again,' they said.' Sadly, I shook my head. 'How could they make me chose one over the other?

'So, I had to make a choice. Peter or my parents. No hard choice really. My body echoed with Peter. It was like, like he had crept under my skin and into my very being.' I hugged myself. 'Peter was here,' I touched my chest. 'Peter was here,' I touched my heart. 'Peter was here,' I held my head, my arms, my legs. 'Peter consumed me.'

'My parents were true to their word. I was not allowed back into my childhood home. When Peter was away, I only had to touch a part of me, and he was there, wherever I was. I had food poisoning when Peter arrived home that last time. I didn't know that the pill wouldn't work. I fell pregnant with Brian. Peter returned back to the oil rigs. Then it was just one phone call to me. He didn't give me a number to ring, so I couldn't contact him. I gave birth to Brian in the hospital.' My face darkened. 'I was told I had to leave the flat by a solicitor when Brian was three months old.'

I fell silent. I stood up and walked out towards the sleeping fox, envying its simple life. After a few minutes I returned to sit near Michael. I turned toward him.

'That is the story of Peter. He is still inside me; he is part of my very being. He gave me a ring before he left. It was inscribed 'You are my only one.' I never met him again. My parents refused to look at their only grandson. Social services found me a flat where Brian and I lived till Brian was ten. My parents died unexpectedly. They left me a sizeable amount of money, so I was able to buy a small house for the two of us.'

After some minutes, 'I kept the ring because I always believed he would come back.' I watched Michael's face. 'I was so very wrong.' I looked down at my hands that were tearing up a napkin. 'How do you wash a man out of your very being?' Michael made no comment. I stood up again and walked round the garden. When I returned to the table Michael had gone, along with the coffee cups. I sighed, 'Men!' Then sat to watch the sleeping fox.

Margery, I learned, was one of the carers appointed to me, came to take me to the day room where drinks were being handed out. Like Margery, most of the staff wore jeans with loose top. Margery had dark hair and blue eyes, so matched her top in blue. A very chatty lady with a humorous face was handing out drinks. I was surprised at the room. Light, airy, simply furnished with a tea bar open for us to order our drinks. The small unit catered for twelve adults, ranging from early twenties to a couple of older ladies and gentlemen.

I asked for my coffee then walked to a table by the window. A young woman came and sat by me. Vivid eyes, pale face, slim.

I asked, 'Have you been here long?' A silent shake of the head from her.

Margery came across. 'Lisa doesn't speak to anyone, so the shake of the head means you are special'. Turning to me, she said, 'Is there anyone you would like us to contact, Val?'

'Janice, I must've scared her silly.' Putting my cup on the table, I stood up.

'Stay there Val, Janice has phoned a couple of times and hopes to visit in a couple of days. She's been called back into work.' Keeping her eyes on my face, she continued, 'There is a man who has called. He said you do not know him, but he would like to speak with you. He said he is Peter's father and has been trying to trace you for a long time.'

I stilled. 'Peter's father? I don't think we ever met. I don't know. No, not just now. Why does he want to speak to me?' I looked up at Margery.

Margery pulled out a chair taking hold of my left hand as she sat down. 'What we can arrange is for you to see him for ten minutes with a member of staff present.'

'No, I am not sure. Why would he want to speak to me?'

'You won't know unless you see him, will you?'

I look across at the silent Lisa, who just stares at me. I notice a slight flicker in her eyes.

'OK, I will see him, but only for ten minutes. Something tells me they lived abroad, Peter's parents.'

'Don't worry Val, someone will be there for you. Dr Michael has scheduled you a spot each day you are here. We are hoping you will go home next week.' With that, Margery left to speak to others needing her.

I look at Lisa. 'Why now?' I fiddle with my hands. 'Why now? I haven't heard from Peter since before Brian was born. It's very strange. What do you think, Lisa?' I thought I saw a ghost of a smile on her face, but it appeared and disappeared so quickly I could not be sure. Finishing my coffee, I asked, 'Shall we walk in the garden? A fox was sleeping amongst the trees. Shall we go and see if it is still there?'

Lisa looked interested when I mentioned the fox. We took our cups back to the counter before slipping out of the door to walk round the garden. The fox had gone, but there was an indentation in the ground where he had lain.

A few days later, I was shown into a small sitting room. Little furniture, just enough to give a homely feel. Easy chairs round a coffee table. Sat in one of the chairs looking out onto the garden was a man with short white hair. He was bouncing his keys up and down in his right hand while holding something in his left. Margery asked if we would like coffee or tea, with cake or biscuits.

The man shot onto his feet, his eyes meeting mine quizzically. He slowly unwound to his full height, then looked at his left hand, bringing it up to his shoulder. A slow smile spread over his face. He put whatever was in his left hand in a pocket as he reached out his right hand to shake mine, holding it in both hands warmly and gently. I smiled as his hair, not as thick as it once was, fell over his left eye as Peter's used to. 'You're Val. I have heard a bit about you. I don't know why you are in this place, but I am sure we can get you out fast. I am Peter's father. My name is Peter too, but I am usually called Pete, so please call me Pete.' Pete looked at the chairs. 'Peter always talks about you.' Still holding my hand, he led me to a small settee. 'Val! Val, at long last I have found you.' His eyes, grey blue, never leaving my face.

Coffee arrived, it smelt lovely, but I was mesmerised by Peter's father. He was so like Peter, older, wiser but Peter in most things he did. He passed me a coffee. 'Peter says you like it sweet, is that still how you like it?' he asked passing me the sugar bowl.

'No, not anymore, just half a spoonful is wonderful. How did you find me? Where is Peter?'

His face clouded over. 'I am sorry Val,' his eyes went to the garden. 'Peter cannot come to you. I will tell you what I know, then you must decide.' He looked at my pale, tensed face.

'Peter was staying in North London. He was doing well for himself. Every time we saw him, he mentioned a girl he had met.' He smiled at me. 'He was going back to the rigs telling me that the next time he would bring you to arrange 'our wedding'.

My hands shook. Margery discreetly took the cup, placing it on the table. 'Our Wedding.' I put my hands over my mouth. Pete smiled a small smile.

'He had been working a few weeks and there was an accident. We didn't hear about it for a while.' Pete paused taking in a few deep breaths. 'When we heard, he was in hospital, not expected to live.'

Val felt a stab in her heart, 'Not live?'

'Yes, that is what we were told.' Pete looked out of the window. Still looking at the window he continued 'We took a train up there, then a cab to the hospital. It was the worst moment in our lives. He. He was trussed up with wires everywhere.'

The sun was being covered by a cloud, so appropriate just now. I leaned over to Pete and placed a hand on his shoulder. He smiled gently though tears were in his eyes.

'But Peter didn't die. It was six months before he could speak at all. Then mostly we had to learn to hear his words.' Pete shook his head. 'Bad times Val, bad times. We were told he could come home if we had a home suitable for him. We looked at the plans of what he would need, then we looked round for something suitable.' Pete turned back to the room. In the end we found a property in Aldwick that needed lots of repairs, so we bought it, spent money on it and eighteen months later we installed Peter in his own house.'

'Aldwick? Aldwick, that's just down the road from where I live!' I fell silent for a few minutes. 'We were so close... but so far away too. How sad. How very sad! If only I had known.' I looked at Pete.

'Well, we eventually understood from Peter that his girlfriend needed to be told. The flat belonged to a company, that is why you were asked to leave. With no money going into that account, the rent was not being paid. Pete looked at me. 'I am sorry Val, if we had known.' Pete looked at the floor then back at me.

'I looked in the area where you used to live. We found out where your parents lived, but they denied your existence. We went back several times. Why did they disown you?'

'Because I moved in with Peter as an unmarried woman. To my parents that was the worst thing that could happen, unless I became pregnant, which I did.'

'That was hard.'

'My parents placed too much importance on 'what the neighbours would say.' I shrugged my shoulders. 'They missed Brian's formative years. Brian did not take to them at all.'

'They came round, then.'

'Dad knocked on my door when Brian was eight. 'He said he had looked into my life and at how many men I had had.' I gritted my teeth. 'He asked me to visit without Brian as my mother was very ill, then he left.

'A few weeks later, when Brian was at a birthday party, I visited them. Mum was ill, she died a few weeks later. Dad followed her three months after that.' I looked at Pete. 'My parents thought they would never have children, but I came along when Mum was in her mid-forties. It must have been hard for them to bring up a child at that age. Anyway, they had some money tucked away which they left to me. It was enough for me to buy a small house for Brian and me. So, I guess some good came out of it.'

'Did you move far?'

'No, not more than a few miles.' I smiled 'We thought we had come up in the world, a private estate! Me, a sinner with a child and no obvious support than what I worked for. I had one good neighbour though, we had coffee occasionally.' Pete suddenly looked up.

'I think my half hour is up. Probably more than up. I understand you will not be here for long, Val.' He took out an envelope. 'When you are ready, please do get in touch. I am sure Peter would like to meet up.' He stood up, giving me the envelope. As I turned round, I saw Dr Michael at the door ready to escort him out.

I put the envelope in my pocket as I walked to the opposite door, which opened onto a patio area. I was shortly joined by Dr Michael, who led me to a wooden stained bench with a similar table in front of it. Margery brought us out cold drinks, joining us at the table.

'All these years and he is alive and not married. He did wait for me.' I picked up my glass of orange, lime and something I could not place. I took several sips before putting it on the table. 'He really loves me.' I shuddered. 'He didn't abandon me.' Then the tears flowed once more. These were tears of happiness.

Later I found Lisa. We walked round the garden as I told her the love of my life is alive. 'I just have to see him.' Lisa turned to face me, her eyes smiling with tears. She gave me a big hug.

'I am pleased for you, Val,' she whispered in my ear. I held her at arm's length. 'Lisa, you have a lovely voice, please use it more often.'

She smiled, whispering, 'Yes perhaps I will.' We walked on a few yards. 'Val, if you can sort your life out after all these years, I should be able to sort mine out. You have given me hope.'

We walked back to the unit bathed in smiles.

I was considered fit enough to go home within a couple of days. Dr Michael gave me a card with his phone number on it. 'Ring if the red mist starts to descend.' I smiled and thanked everyone at the unit, promising to visit soon. Janice collected me on the Wednesday evening, returning to my home with me.

Janice bubbled over, 'You are so different Val, the change is enormous. Though it scared me, I'm glad it all happened. It was something you have needed.'

'Thanks Janice, there is so much for me to tell you, give me a few days and I will cook for you and tell you so many wonderful things. It is the best that has happened to me, though I am sorry for that lady and child.'

Janice hugged me. 'I'll ring tomorrow.'

I returned to work on the Monday. Everything was the same, but I was different. At the weekend I opened the envelope Pete had given me with his phone number on it. We agreed to meet up in 'London Road' café for a light bite to eat. I love their prawn and salmon salad; Pete ordered a burger and chips. We sat upstairs in the quieter area. Pete asked if Brian could join us. I stilled, watching his face. I took a deep breath and nodded. Pete took out his phone spoke to Brian and agreed he would arrive as we finished our meal. I was jittery. Could we bury the past?

Pete watched my face and the emotions travelling over it. 'Val, if you are to heal properly you need to resolve all your issues.'

I nodded, 'Yes, you're right.' We chatted about this and that as we ate our meals, then Pete went down to order more coffee. He returned with Brian who also had a coffee. Pete put the tray on the table. I looked up at Brian.

'Brian do sit down; I really don't bite.' Brian smiled. Sitting opposite me. 'Mum,' he stopped, looking deep into my eyes. 'I am sorry, you were right, Ruth was a bad one. We were going to get married at the registry office. She didn't show, though two police officers did. Ruth had been stealing, that is when I found out about the rings. Mum, I am really sorry.'

I smiled. 'I need to say sorry too Brian. I lost it when your wife showed me the box. I ended up in hospital with mental illness for the second time.' I took a sip of my coffee, then looked at Brian. 'Do you think we could help each other to put it all behind us?' Brian gave me a big hug. We both cried. Presently, my grandson Peter came cautiously to sit by us. Brian introduced us, and when Pam, his wife arrived, I apologised.

'No need Val. I went too fast; it was partly my fault. Let's start again, my name is Pam and I am married to a wonderful man called Brian, whose mother has had a rough ride, and we would both like to make her life easier. We have a son, whose name is Peter.'

'And Peter wants a grandmother,' Peter shouted, then looked at me. 'Would you be my grandmother?'

'I'd love to be your grandmother Peter. Now I need to find your grandfather.'

Peter looked earnestly into my eyes. 'I have a grandfather and a great grandfather. Would you like to meet my grandfather? He can't walk far but you could come and visit him when we go.'

'I'd love that Peter; shall we say next weekend?'

Peter thought about that while wringing his hands as his father always did when thinking. 'I'll ask him, then Granddad Pete can ring you.' He turned towards Pete. 'You would do that, ask granddad if grandma can visit?'

Pete smiled, 'Yes, Peter, I am sure we can arrange something.'

A week later I was collected and taken to Peter's home, a large, older property glinting in the sun, within its own grounds. I walked up to the blue door which opened as I went to knock. Pam gave me a hug. 'We are having lunch in the conservatory; I'll take you through. '

This might be a house for an invalid, but it didn't look like one. We walked through and my Brian was in there. Brian, his father and Brian's son, all from the same pod. All their hair fell over their left eyes. Their heads tipped to the same angle to the right. They all raised their right arms to make a point. I stood spellbound.

Pam laughed, 'It's a bit like the three wise monkeys, though I doubt about the 'wise' bit.'

They all looked up. Peter's eyes locked with mine; the chemistry was still there. No-one else in the room was there, just the two of us. Neither of us heard them leave; we were in our own bubble. Slowly Peter stood up.

'Val, you have no idea how long it has taken Dad and me to find you.' He took one slow step, then another, before losing his balance, grabbing the table. I ran to catch him. 'Sorry, I need a walking stick or two,' he looked round him on the floor. 'Peter likes to use them for other things.

'Val,' his hands went to my face, then slowly stroked first down the sides of my face then playfully down my nose. He gently tilted my head to place a gentle kiss on my lips. We were lost in each other as we had always been. We sank slowly onto Peter's seat, our arms wrapped round each other.

We heard a little voice. 'Do you think they will get married now they've kissed?'

'Hush,'

'Well, he has the ring, we only need a priest.'

Peter and I laughed against each other. Then Peter asked, 'Shall we get married, my Val?'

With tears streaming down my face, I replied 'We've kissed, so I think we had better.' I nestled my head into Peter's shoulder, and he placed his head on mine.

Dreams are sometimes repeated over many months or even years. The first paragraph and the first sentence of the second paragraph of the following story is my recurring dream. The rest is fiction. It is said to dream of houses is to dream of yourself!

A Recurring Dream

I am walking down a road at dusk, looking at houses with dull lights yet to reach their full brightness. Turning a corner, I am surprised to see one house larger than the rest, sparkling through the gathering darkness. I smile at the coloured lights round the eaves and shining out of the lower casement windows. The upstairs windows shimmer with a soft, gentle warmth.

Walking towards this house, I am transported into the attic, where I stand looking round me at the muddle that occupies the space. The attic is crammed with boxes of all shapes and sizes. None appear to have labels on them. Looking down at myself, I have reverted to my ten-year-old self, dressed in a knee-length navy skirt with a navy school jumper. My feet have black lace-up shoes over knee-high socks. My hair is a plain bob, brushed to one side. The small number of visible floorboards are light wood. My ten-year-old self is searching for something, finding a box; a small white box not much larger than a necklace box. Pushing the boxes aside to create a larger space, then falling down cross-legged in the space on the boarded floor, I lift the lid cautiously. Inside is an ancient war horse, its head peeping out of tissue paper. Placing the box on the floorboards, I gently lift the little horse out to hold gently in my hands. It is as I remembered it as a small child: the horse with its chipped white paint, its tattered saddle and broken tail.

As I smile sadly, I can see myself in our family home with my brother Peter, playing war games with horses, cannons and fences, Peter lecturing me about strategy, how I always seem to have my 'army' out of order. How patient he was with his five-year-old sister, wanting her to be the best commander of them all. He always ended up saying 'remember this: Don't ask anyone to do something you would not do yourself. There is nothing wrong in scrubbing, cleaning, tidying, even cleaning toilets. It is all part of life. Please sis, remember. It's important.'

Silent tears rolled down my face as I remember how he suddenly passed out as we played our last war game together. I screamed, running for Mum, still holding this horse in my hand. Both our parents ran into the room while I stood at the door watching. Pandemonium set in. A doctor called. A neighbour led me into her house. Gently, Mrs Bental ushered me into her parlour, seating me in a chair by a laid fire that would not have a light put to it for many months yet.

A glass of lemonade arrived in my right hand. A homemade bun was offered from her plump hands, still warm from the baking trays from her double oven; I knew these would be iced later. I sat still, holding the little horse in my left hand. Together the horse and I waited in Mrs Bental's parlour while I sipped the lemonade slowly, trying to keep the fear away.

'What is happening to my army commander?' I whispered to the little horse. 'Will he be alright? He probably didn't eat any breakfast. Mum will be cross with him, you wait and see.' Several screams filtered into the parlour. Mrs Bental brought her chair to mine, placing her warm arm round my shoulders and whispered, I know not what, in my ears.

My Aunt May arrived in Mrs Bental's parlour to take me to her home some miles away. Silently I walked with her. Aunt May thanked Mrs Bental for taking care of me before she sat me in the back of her car. I looked at my home. Door open wide, doctor on the doorstep with his big black bag shaking my Father's hand, my Mother nowhere to be seen. Father did not notice I was in a car, being carried away. Still gripping my little horse, I knelt on the seat hoping for a wave. Hoping Father would run after the car, shouting 'Come back with my daughter, everything is fine.'

Aunt May found me this box to wrap the little horse in. My cousin Lilly found the tissue paper. It was kept by my bed for months, at least that was how it seemed to a five-year-old. It was a month, though, before I returned to the now sombre house. Aunt May told me my brother would not be there. He had died unexpectedly. 'Be a good girl for your parents, try to help them Susan.'

Father had gone off on business and would not be home for several months. I took myself to school, joining the class I had left. My teacher, Mrs White, a tall slim lady of similar age to my mother, kept me in after school for an hour twice a week to help me catch up. I worked hard on the homework she gave me, returning it the following morning, revelling in her smile of praise. This would be the only interaction I would receive during my days, as mother rarely left her room.

A housekeeper-come-cook was employed, living in the rooms attached to the kitchen. Mrs Keen called me one Saturday morning, asking if I would like to help her. I felt such joy as I had entered the kitchen lit by the warm summer sun. The air was perfumed with smells of yeast and honey, while a lamb hot-pot simmered on the stove. This lovely lady, her almost black hair in a bun at the back of her neck, brought happiness into my weekend world. She brought out a second apron that she managed to 'fit' with folds before tying it around my skinny waist. I stood on a low stool as she taught me how to weigh ingredients and then to sieve the flour, how to start the yeast off and to soak the dried fruit in tea to 'plump them up'. With Mrs Keen, I learned all the basics of cooking and carefully wrote out all the recipes in my own cooking folder. I lived for weekends. Mrs Keen and Mrs White were the two people I flourished under.

Aunt May came regularly to the house, going straight to Mother's room. She would stay for two hours longer on a Saturday. I would make tea and scones for them, which Mrs Keen would take upstairs, asking me to follow her. Aunt May always came to the door to take the tray. Always she gave me a big smile and whispered she would be down soon.

Mrs Keen and I returned to the kitchen to eat our scones and drink lemonade. Aunt May came down, bringing the tray with her. Taking a seat at the table and turning to me, she asked to see my homework. Eventually the day came that I told I did not have any, as I had now caught up with the rest of the class.

She beamed into my troubled face. 'Well done Susan!' A big hug came my way. 'I can see you will go far.' Returning to Mrs Keen, 'How are the cookery lessons going Mrs Keen?'

'Really well, if she carries on, I can see myself out of a position,' Mrs Keen replied, smiling at me. 'She is turning into a good little cook. She helped me with today's hotpot. Susan, bring one of your books down for your Aunty to see how well you are doing at school.'

I climbed down from my chair, knowing they wanted time together. So, I took a long time finding my book, taking out my little horse and speaking to Peter, telling them both the praise I had received.

Father came home, staying a couple of months before returning to far-flung places. Before leaving, father reminded me not to disturb my mother! A nurse was added to the household, though I rarely saw her flitting up the stairs in her blue nurse outfit. Still, I had Mrs Keen at home and Mrs White, who in time morphed into Mr Peek, then Mrs Tissel, then Mrs Smith, and now Mr Thomas, a dour but fair man who pushed his pupils harshly. We all were given some homework of sorts to prepare for the '11+'. Fingers crossed, I hoped to pass.

Father came home my eleventh summer. He called me into his study, his thin frame looking out of place in the large leather chair he had filled when Peter was alive. 'Susan, as you know, your mother is not well. The doctor advises she is taken somewhere warm to live for a while. I have made arrangements for you to go to a boarding school outside of Maidenhead. Mrs Keen will stay here to take care of the house where you will stay in the school holidays. It was your Mother's school, and she always spoke well of it. You will leave here at the end of August. Mrs Keen will help to buy your uniform and anything else you need. She is a good woman, Mrs Keen.' Father paused here turning away. I watched as his face contorted. Finally, he looked towards me. 'She, Mrs Keen, will visit you each term.'

Tentatively I asked, 'When will you and Mother leave?'

'Friday next week.' For the first time he truly looked at me. 'Susan, I am really sorry... You have had a rough five years. I hope your mother will recover soon.' He paused, deep in thought. 'Peter always thought you were the clever one. Don't let him or yourself down. Mrs Keen is waiting to take you into town.' As I turned to close the door, I looked back to see father slumped in his chair, eyes shut, with tears falling silently down his tired face.

I am walking down a road at dusk, looking at houses with dull lights yet to reach their full brightness. Turning a corner, I am surprised to see one house larger than the rest, sparkling through the gathering darkness. I smile at the coloured lights round the eaves and shining out of the lower casement windows. The upstairs windows shimmer with a soft, gentle warmth.

Walking towards this house I am transported into the attic, where I stand looking round me taking stock. The attics have many boxes of all shapes and sizes. None appear to have labels on them. I am dressed in my unflattering, brown senior school uniform. The only interesting bit of it is the elaborate crest on the jacket pocket and the gold braid edging. My matching hat with its narrow brim and brown chin ties is hanging from my hand.

There are fewer boxes than the last time I was here. The wooden floor looks as though it has been recently polished, though with what, I cannot say. There is no perfume to enlighten me. In the middle of the floor lies a package wrapped in brown paper. I walk over to it, dropping my hat to the floor as I sit down, pulling the loosely tied string dragging the package close to me. Slipping off my brown court shoes, now in stockinged feet I sit cross-legged in front of the package. It is old, the string yellowing. I untie the string, carefully winding it up. I lay the package with the joins face up, with a mixture of emotions in my churning stomach and mildly shaking hands. As the paper comes apart, there is a stack of envelopes wrapped in a white document. I lift the document and run my thumb through the envelopes, all addressed in my own handwriting; all with the post office franking dates.

I am confused. Opening out the document I start to read it.

'Dear Susan,

When you receive this package, it will be because you understand better what has happened. As you know, I took your mother away to warmer climes to heal. Unfortunately, she died last month on the 5th of February; the doctors said of heart failure. I fear she never recovered from Peter's death. I am so very sorry that many of your letters are unopened. Since her death I have not had the heart to read anything.

I have been in touch with your headmistress Mrs Lincoln, who tells me you are an excellent pupil and should go to university if you wish, to complete a maths degree. I am so very proud of you and have asked Mrs Lincoln to hold back this news till you have completed your 'O' levels. I will be able to collect you from school at the end of term, as I am making plans to return to England and our home permanently. I have badly neglected you and wish dearly to make up for the loss of time.

'Your loving Father'.

I place the letter on the floor beside me. I had had a scary feeling that many of my letters were unopened. I now lift them onto my lap. I feel desperately sad that over months and months my weekly letters were not opened. I feel neglected, rejected even.

Unaware, I have drifted into my boarding school classroom, when our lesson is interrupted as a secretary is asking me to accompany her to the headmistress' office. Wondering what I had done so very wrong, as interviews with Mrs Lincoln were usually after classes but before dinner, puzzled and bewildered, I walk silently with her to the school office.

I wait outside the head mistresses office while her secretary, Miss Andrews, with her permed hair, announces I have arrived. Mrs Lincoln comes to greet me as I enter, a most unusual thing for her to do. Her light brown hair bobbed to just above the shoulder with her pearl necklace lying on her beige twin set, she shakes my hand, putting her left arm round my shoulder to lead me to the low burning fire, where three chairs had been drawn up. As I am seated, I see Mrs Keen. Getting up and showing joy I rush to her. The dear lady gives me a big hug while tears run down her face. I kneel at her knee. 'Whatever is the matter?' I hug her again. The tears slow, then stop, but her shoulders still shake.

Mrs Lincoln bids me sit in a seat next to her. While Mrs Keen recovers, she tells me of my Mother's demise. I cannot shed any tears. It is more than ten years since I last set eyes on her. She was a figure who lived in a bedroom near mine; she had taken no interest in my wellbeing. Mrs Keen was more of a mother to me. I reach out and hold Mrs Keen's hand. Eventually we are given tea and biscuits. Mrs Lincoln begins to talk about my going home early for Easter, but I don't want to. I need the company of my room mates.

Mrs Keen understands, stating she will collect me in two weeks' time, that I can help her 'sort' Father's bedroom and to 'think of any ideas'. I return to my classroom, but have trouble concentrating on my work. The teachers are very kind to me, as were all the rest of the girls.

I return home with Mrs Keen in due course. Together we clear my parents' room. Father had sent money to Mrs Keen for any replacements she thought were suitable. We eagerly ditch the old bed covers, spending a great deal of time chasing new bedding, curtains and bedside rug. Some of my Mother's clothes left in the wardrobe go to the Salvation Army, as does the better bed linen.

Mrs Keen brings in a decorator she knows, and we choose new wall and ceiling colours. The room will be 'as new'. Together we hope Father will like the changes.

All too soon I return to school, though with a lighter heart. The house looked better, and next time I arrive home my Father will be there.

Father is at school to collect me a week after my exams. I will be notified of the results by post. Father looks so thin, so pale, so very old; his face seems devoid of emotion. His jacket and trousers seem to hang off his skinny frame. He is not the father my five-year-old self remembered. Mrs Keen is waiting in the car to drive us home. Father insists we stop for an expensive tea to celebrate his coming home and the end of my exams.

Back in the attic, I carefully wrap the unopened letters up, loosely tying the string. I still feel neglected by my parents. I have Mrs Keen, who I have come to love, realising she is not much younger than my father and wishing she could be my official mum.

I am walking down a road at dusk, looking at houses with dull lights yet to reach their full brightness. Turning a corner, I am surprised to see one house larger than the rest, sparkling through the gathering darkness. I smile at the lights round the eaves and shining out of the casement windows. The upstairs windows shimmer with soft, gentle warmth.

Walking towards this house I am transported into the attic, where I stand looking round me taking stock. The attic has fewer boxes, though many shapes and sizes. A large part of the floor has been cleared of the boxes from previous visits. In some disjointed way I wonder what has become of them. Shrugging my shoulders as I walk to a stack of boxes under one of the east eaves. I run my hand up and down the boxes in a careless way. The boxes look as though they are filled with books.

Pulling out the top box, sealed with parcel wrap that is rather fragile, I take it to the centre of the attic. Removing my low-heeled shoes, I sit loosely cross-legged on the floor, under the small electric light bulb hanging above. I had helped Father put in the light, if only by holding on to the stepladder. Patting my jeans down I lift the box to sit between my knees. Gently I pull off the old parcel tape, the lid coming too. Carefully wrapped in paper is my maid of honour hat; pale pink silk flowers surrounded with white silk petals, round a palest green, narrow-brimmed hat with a net to hide under or to roll back on top. I cannot resist putting it on my head, letting the small veil cover part of my face and smiling at the recollection.

I have somehow returned to my family home. Father is standing tall, a glass in hand by a warm fire, even though it is summer, his frame having filled out, giving him a younger look and a sparkle back in his eyes. I have finished my 'A' levels, coming home to wait the results. Father and Mrs Keen are a couple, complete with an engagement ring. We go to a hotel for a celebration with lots of friends known to both of them, joining in the noon lunch and remaining for afternoon tea. A quartet plays all afternoon. It is such wonderful fun. Mrs Keen is truly going to be my 'mummy'. The big day is to follow quickly, as neither of them want to wait. The wedding itself is to be a quiet affair in the local church, just close family, and a quiet supper in an out of town restaurant.

Mrs Keen is going to wear a silk dress and jacket, Father his black suit and red bow tie. I am to get my first real grown-up outfit. Mrs Keen searches out many dresses for me to try on, deliberately insisting I try on outfits that are so unsuitable. Giggling, I try them all on. We settle on a floral dress, nipped in at the waist with floating sleeves from the elbows, accompanied with light green waist jacket of summer weight linen. We choose matching bag, shoes and hat. The chosen hat is decorated with pale blue and white silk flowers in a circle round its wider brim.

Many not invited to the reception arrive at the church to wish them well. One of Father's old work colleagues stands in as best man, and one of Mrs Keen's brothers stands in to escort her 'down the aisle'. It is a simple service without a choir or bells and only one hymn. Both have been widowed, so neither wanted a fancy affair.

Outside the church people line the path from the church doors to the cars taking us to the restaurant. Both Mrs Keen and Father have a wide circle of friends who want to wish them well on their big day. It is an emotional moment, bringing tears to my eyes at the love surrounding them.

At the restaurant we are shown into a side room, with tables laid fitting the occasion. Fresh flowers sit on circular tables, eenabling everyone to see each other. Waiting staff serve all tables at the same time. It's fascinating to see it all happening. Staff in black and white gliding in a wave both to the tables and to the kitchens, returning to stand in their places like guards at Buckingham Palace. What we ate is a blur, but I can see clearly the two tiered cake I had made, the bottom layer of fruit, the top of vanilla sponge all covered in white icing and decorated with blue, cream and pale pink flowers made from icing. I smile as I remember the hours I spent hiding at Aunt May's house so I could surprise my new parents.

The day goes really well, and we send the happy couple off in confetti. I stay with Aunt May for a week before leaving to start my accountancy course at uni…

I smile down at the hat with its faded flowers. Reluctantly, I cover it in tissue, to return to its box.

I am walking down a road at dusk, looking at houses with dull lights yet to reach their full brightness. Turning a corner, I am surprised to see one house larger than the rest, sparkling through the gathering darkness. I smile at the lights round the eaves and shining out of the casement windows. The upstairs windows shimmer with soft, gentle warmth. As I walk towards the house, I am transported to the attic.

The floor looks newly polished, giving off a slight glow. I walk lightly towards the south corner of the eaves, where an untidy pile of boxes sits, precariously balanced. The light from the window seemed to have faded some of the wooden floor, giving it an appearance of having received a light caramel coat. An old wooden rocking chair is sat under the unlit light bulb. In my jeans, I kneel by the pile of packages, fingering the boxes lightly. I pick up a small package before returning to laze in the rocking chair. The small package was white, but is now yellowed to almost parchment colour. I lazily turn it over in my hand, trying to figure what is inside the package.

There is no tape round this box, so, I carefully raise the lid. Inside is a red ring box. I place a hand over the O my mouth is making. As I rock back and forth for a few minutes, my carpet slippered feet on the wooden floor, memories of a difficult time flood back. I am in a shared flat close to the university, where I met Graham; tall, good-looking in a rugged way, hair seeming wild, dark brown eyes and deep sensual lips hiding good white teeth and a comedic tongue. He has dimples that bring laughter to my lips when he smiles. Graham is also studying Accountancy, though he's two years ahead of me and hopes to become a chartered accountant in nine months' time, following in his father's business.

We have set up in this flat together, sharing the chores, though Graham liked doing most of the cooking. He's into cricket, so in the season, we eat out after the weekend games. Most of the team and their partners all meet up at an out of town pub for an evening of hilarity. Graham comes from a family of teetotallers, and as I rarely drink anything other than tea and water it suits us both. We become engaged after Graham met my parents, who he gets along well with. His parents live overseas, so we meet them when uni is out for the summer, meeting up in their home on the outskirts of Brighton.

During our last stay in Brighton, Graham introduces me to a slim blonde in his year. Leslie is as tall as Graham, living not far from his family home. They had been in their first school together and both sets of parents were friends. Leslie doesn't hide the confidence that oozes out of her skin. She comes across as predatory, keeping an arm on her current beau but pushing herself across all other men in the room.

Graham's parents are lovely, making me feel quite at home and introducing me to many people my own age. We play an interpretation of tennis on the lawn after having four-o'clock tea! The weekend flies by, and with Graham mostly by my side we laugh and giggle through from morning to night.

Charles and Martha, Graham's parents, stay in touch at least monthly, though frequently more often. I believe Graham is having extra sessions with his tutor till, out shopping for our supper one Thursday, I see him with Leslie, arms round each other, going into a pub for lunch. At first disbelief stops me in my tracks.

Heavy bag in my left hand dropping to the floor, my right hand drops its shopping list to cover the silent NO my mouth is making. A concerned stranger stops to check I'm OK; gathering up my packages and my list before taking my arm, he leads me to a pavement café to sit me down. He orders a coffee, insisting I drink it with loads of sugar.

Eventually the shock eases and I look into the light brown eyes of this man. He wears the clothes of a carpenter, brown dungarees over a checked shirt, his muscled arms covered in a dusting of wood shavings while his hair is peppered with wood dust so the colour could not be presumed. I manage a smile through tears that had started to fall. His hands, slim through work, gently take a couple of tissues off the table to put in my hands.

He sits with me till he's sure I'm fine, then walks me back to our flat a few streets away. As we reach the flat door, Graham comes up the road in a fluster, rushing up to me.

'Are you OK?' He looks at the intruder.

I speak quickly. 'I had a shock outside the 'Wagon Wheel' and this kind generous man bought me a coffee before bringing me home safely.'

He smiles at the intruder, holding out his hand to shake it, when he realises what I've said. Turning back to me, 'You... You were outside the Wagon Wheel?'

'Yes, Graham, I was outside the Wagon Wheel.' I turn to open the door. Graham walks through it.

Turning back to the carpenter, though sad, I manage a smile and a big thank you, before asking if we could meet up again so I could return the favour. His open smile cheers me. 'I would like that.' He looks inside the door at Graham's retreating back. 'Yes, that would be nice. I am working in the Wagon Wheel at the moment, so just pop down the alley way and shout for Steve.' With that he walks away. Turning, I walk into the flat gently closing the door after me.

Graham is packing his clothes. Briskly, he tells me, 'The rent is paid till the end of the summer term.' He looks up at me with a sadness I did not expect. 'Sue.' He shakes his head and strokes his chin. Turned to look out of the window before returning his gaze to me. 'Sue, I am so very sorry, Leslie and I spent a weekend together while you were visiting your parents. She just told me she is pregnant. I have made an enormous mistake.' He walks towards me then wraps his arms round my limp body. 'If only... If only I could turn the clock back.' He rocks me silently for a long time. 'She is not a patch on you, but her parents have been in touch with mine. While in the pub, my parents rang. I either marry her or they will cut me off with no prospects of a job either.' A long deep sigh. 'It is a mistake I will have to live with for the rest of my life.' He holds me closer. 'What a fool I have been. You and I were meant for each other and I blew it with that dense bitch!'

He lays his head on my shoulder, snuggling into my neck. 'Sue, I will never forgive myself for what I have done to us.' I can feel his tears rolling down my neck. I finally raise my arms round his shoulders, as I would have done for Peter. How long we stay like this I do not know, though long enough for the room to dim into dusk and on into evening. His phone rings, and with a reluctance I could feel he untangles himself, taking the call from one of his parents. He walks into our kitchen and I hear;

'Yes, I have just told her.'

Gently, I take the lovely engagement ring off my finger.

'No, that would be cruel.'

I walk to my cupboard to find the ring box.

'The rent is paid, so leave it be,' this last said on a sob.

I place the ring inside the box.

'Leslie and I will be back later this evening.'

I take off my shoes.

'We thought we would eat on the way. See you then.'

The flat falls silent.

Graham returns to finish his packing. 'I will come for the rest next week when you're at your parents.' He looks into my drained face. 'I am so sorry.' I give him the ring box. He opens it. 'No, no, please keep it. If times are hard you should get a good price for it. I will find the receipt for you and leave it with a letter.' He glances round the bedroom bereft. 'Oh, Sue!'

He grabs his bag, leaving in a whirlwind.

As the echo of his footsteps fade behind a slammed door, I fall silently onto our bed.

I am walking down a road at dusk, looking at houses with dull lights yet to reach their full brightness. Turning a corner, I am surprised to see one house larger than the rest, sparkling through the gathering darkness. I smile at the lights round the eaves and shining out of the casement windows. The upstairs windows shimmer with a soft, gentle warmth. As I walk towards the house, I am transported to the attic. Dressed in soft sandals on bare feet, loose linen trousers and a matching blouse, I smile as I walk round the attic. Slowly, I am covered in mist, which dissolves outside a flat in a low rise of four storeys.

I have finished uni, taking a position in a small business. Father gave me the deposit to put on this flat. It needs quite a bit of work doing to it. I ask a neighbour if they can recommend someone.

'Yes,' The elderly gentleman says, 'I am going near there now. A young man set up a couple of years ago. He is good, really good. If you have time now I'll take you as I am going in his direction.' So, I walk with him down the road turning into an entrance of an alley near our block of flats. 'The short way,' the gentleman, who tells me his name is Barry, stops after about five minutes to point down another alley. 'You'll find him down there.' Barry smiles, then leaves me.

Walking into the workshop, I call, 'Hello?' into the empty building. As the silence settles round me I walk towards an unfinished chest, its lid waiting to be fixed. I run my hand gently over its smooth exterior, a sigh of pleasure running through me.

'Sorry, I was busy outside can I…' I turn to look into the brown eyes of my rescuer.

'Steve,' comes unbidden from my lips.

'Sue.' Silence envelops us. Somehow, we are together. Not touching, but so close, breathing in the scent of the other. Our eyes are locked, each staring deeply at the other's soul. Both raise our arms and then…we are truly together as our lips touch, a very gentle touch, then apart.

With my fingers I gently touch his generous lips.

He takes my fingers, kissing them so gently, with a warmth I have not felt before.

'Steve?' came a shout.

He raises his fingers to my lips. 'Mmmmm.'

'Coffee?'

We both shake ourselves with a smile. Turning, I see Barry with a grin all over his face. 'A nice coffee shop just along the road. Go on, the pair of you,' he hands me my bag, which I had dropped, unnoticed.

Back in the attic I rock the crib Steve spent hours making, used for all four of our children, look at the little horse. The rocking chair he made so I could feed the babies in comfort. I sit for a few minutes to look at the clay vase made by Mary at school. Little Steve made the jewellery box in woodwork, also at school. Now he is at uni, studying to become a doctor.

Sam is training to become a dressmaker, and her tailor's dummies have various homes round the attic, in various states of dress. An apprenticeship has been offered after her college course, which she is so looking forward to. Brian is studying for his 'A's but is unsure which route to take.

Sadly, Father died a few years ago, after many happy years with Mummy, who is a resident in a nursing home, though locally, so I can visit every day. Steve's parents are moving house to be closer to us and their grandchildren. My attic is now clean and filled with lovely memories, much laughter and an extraordinary, loving husband who is so clever at keeping me warm, feeling loved and wanted.

I take one last look round the attic, stopping to take another look at the little lead horse once more. As I do, I can hear Peter's voice.

'Well done sis. I am really proud of you. I always knew you would get there.'

I thought I saw the horse move. 'No, no.' I give myself a little shake as I turn to leave the attic with lots of love and laughter in my heart.

A Good Turn

I grew up as the only child in the family. I was not a particularly bright child, though my parents did all they could so I would leave school with a reasonable education. Dad worked at a factory working in stainless steel. I worked in an office in the town centre as a typist come Girl Friday, a job I loved, making lots of friends in other areas of the company. Mum had a part time job working in the hairdressers.

One day Dad brought home a lad, about five years older than me, to share our evening meal. The poor chap had been told by his landlady that she needed the room for a family member who was in desperate need. So, Daniel, as he was called, was hoping to use our spare room, 'just for a few weeks'. Mum, who was a soft touch, agreed.

Daniel moved in straight away, having breakfast before going to work; mum making sandwiches the same as Dad's for his lunch. Dinner was always at six, when I arrived home. Dad and Daniel usually arrived home about five to shower and change out of their work clothes, so were always waiting in comfy chairs as I came into the house. After dinner I helped mum with the dishes, before going to my room to phone a friend or get ready to go out.

At first Daniel knocked on my bedroom door if he wanted to speak to me, but gradually he started to walk straight in as though he owned the place. Then he started to criticise the way I kept my room! I became really shirty with him.

'This is my room. Your place is not in it. Get out.' Not that it made any impact on Daniel, in fact it made it worse, as he had a horrible smirk on his face as he left my room.

Not stopping with haunting my bedroom, he started to follow me on the days I met up with the girls from work. I complained bitterly to Mum, then to Dad, but they always replied 'he is watching out for you, nothing more. You should be pleased he cares about you.' I was really angry.

One night I woke up with a feeling that someone was watching me. I sat up but could not see anyone so snuggled down in bed going back to sleep. This happened a number of times. I mentioned it to my friends; they were so concerned one of them gave me a small torch to keep under my pillow. I was unwell on the Thursday going to bed early. About half one I woke up with the feeling I was not alone; turning the torch on, I spotted Daniel.

'What are you doing in my room?' I screamed.

'Just checking you are alright.' he replied.

'Get out, get out now!' I yelled. Dad had woken up. He came to my room to see what was going on.

'He has no right to come into my room!' I screamed.

'I was just making sure she was OK,' he replied.

Dad said to go back to sleep and told Daniel to go to bed. The next morning, I told Mum before I left for work that if Daniel did not stay out of my room, I was leaving home.

'Don't be silly,' she said, 'he is just looking out for you.'

'No mum, I mean it, if he comes into my bedroom just once more, I will move out.'

'I'll speak to Dad and see if he will have a word, dear. Just off you go to work, it will be sorted when you get back.'

I arrived home to a quiet house with a quiet dinner; Daniel had been told to stay out of my room and had gone off in a huff. I just went to my room after I had helped with the dishes. Daniel returned on the Sunday to collect his belongings, saying he had found another room. Mum and Dad wished him well and I thought that was the last I would see of him.

I slept easier in my bed for the next week, then woke again with the feeling I was being watched. As I went to turn on the light a hand clapped over my mouth as he caught my hand.

He whispered in my ear, 'Make a noise and I will slit your throat with a knife'. He dropped my hand so he could put a knife against my throat.

Daniel moved the covers off me then ripped my flimsy night dress with his knife. The light of the moon streaming through the now open curtains showed me he was naked. My eyes widened in fright. A small cry escaped into his hand. He put the knife down enabling him to pick up one of my scarves to tie over my mouth very tightly. Taking several pairs of my tights he tied my hands to the lovely metal frame bedstead. He took another pair of tights, slitting them down the middle with his knife. He took the pillows from under my head to raise my bottom at an angle that suited him before tying my feet to the bottom lower bed frame. When he was satisfied, he turned the light on low so he could see my face, now drained of colour, my brown eyes wide open with fright as I sobbed into my own scarf.

I looked into his evil blue eyes, his face mad with rage as he raped me several times, laughing softly into my face. My eyes watched as he stood, going to the end of the bed to dress before hearing a noise that threw him. He waited behind the door. Someone was using the bathroom. He took my blanket laying it across the bottom of the door. Waited till he heard my parents' door close, then waited another five minutes. Silently, like a cat, he cautiously opened the door throwing the blanket to one side, went down the stairs leaving the house by the front door, closing it quietly.

I could not move, so remained naked, uncovered, till my mother, wondering why I had not come down for my breakfast by eight o'clock, came into my bedroom. Mum called an ambulance asking also for police, the police arriving first. I was rushed to hospital where I stayed for a week, having lost a lot of blood and needed stitching up down below. The doctors were not sure that I would be able to conceive a child if I wanted one in later years.

When I was released from hospital, the police came to the house with a counsellor. They told Dad 'Daniel' was called Shaun. There had been a number of similar rapes, but they had not been able to get enough evidence. This time he had left the knife with fingerprints on it, prints were also on the door and the lamp; DNA was found on my bloodied sheet, along with a split condom. 'Daniel', they hoped, would go to prison for a very long time.

When the police left, Dad gave me a big hug, while he kept saying sorry. 'I should have shown him the door the first time you complained about him walking into your room.' I couldn't blame Dad too much, as the police said he always had copies of the door keys made, so he would have found his way in anyway.

The house was not the same afterwards. No matter how often Mum cleaned it, it always felt uncomfortable and dirty in a different way. Dad finally put it on the market where it sold quite quickly. Our new address is a very modern house with extra security, including cameras. I really do not think my dad will offer another man a room, regardless of the circumstances.

Unfortunately, getting my life back is not as easy as moving home. I pass a nice-looking guy on my way to work. How long will it be before I see a man without being afraid?

My First Real Assignment

I saw the man on leaving my car, seated with his back to the wall of the old pub with its seasoned, exposed, black wooden supports. 'Weathered face, wearing a cheese cutter cap, smoking a pipe. Go gently,' my boss told me. 'Don't rush in and scare him off. Buy a drink. Make small talk.'

I'm Alex, fresh out of uni after finishing a course on journalism. This is my third assignment and the most important one to date. The old man is sat in the sun, leaning against the pub wall, twiddling a pipe in his hands. On the bench in front of him is half a pint of ale, his baccy pouch and a couple of keys, with a small pen knife attached to the key ring.

Walking inside the warm pub, I buy half a pint, don't want to overdo the beer. I take the opportunity to look round its interior, taking in the large log fire, unlit today, but in an impressive ancient grate with its equally ancient roasting rods. A hook hangs to the left of the fire. I stare at the hook from the bar, hoping to see a spot of blood. This was the place of a cruel twist of fate, where a man, not much older than me ... died. A slight shudder ripples through my body as I move my eyes to either side of the grate, where piles of small logs are waiting to be used, later perhaps, when the sun slips behind the trees. Probably not the ones he fell on for the final blow! The floor is covered in an old red carpet, which could hide some of the... the evidence.

Tables are arranged ad hoc with mismatched chairs surrounding them. Some younger people, probably students, are making the most of a sunny day out. The food smells good; though it is served in a different bar, its perfume drifts at least to the bar where I am standing. Going back out in the sunshine, I take up a seat near the old man, who is still playing with his pipe, knocking it on the heavy wooden bench then scraping the bowl with his little knife.

'Nice day?' I ask, as I take a first sip of beer.

No reply, not even a flicker of his eyelids.

Creeping a little closer I ask, 'Are you a regular here?'

A glance from watery grey eyes in a weather-worn face. Just a hint of a nod.

'I'm new here. Been here just a few months. It's a lovely spot.' I wriggle a little to settle better on the wooden seat. 'So pleased I found this pub today...' I pick up the menu off the table. 'Is the food good?' I cross my legs, settling in for a long, relaxed chat, while glancing through the menu.

A grunt from the wrinkled face that had spent long hours working out of doors. He puts his pipe between still generous lips.

'A guy at work said there were an incident here in January. Just gossip I guess?'

He pulls his cheese cutter down over his eyebrows. Sighes looking into a distance only he could see.

Finally, he turns to look at me. 'January snowed here,' speaking through his pipe, then sucks on it, raising his head to watch the smoke rising lazily into the almost still, damp air.

'Snowed January. Had a good log fire then,' muttering through his teeth, which stopped his pipe from falling southward.

'He said someone was stabbed. In there,' I point my shoulder towards the pub behind us. 'Some people just love trouble.'

He folds his arm across a deceptively slim frame. 'Yep. Snowed in January. Had chestnuts, hot chestnuts.' He takes his pipe out of his mouth. Looks at it. Bends forward retrieving some matches from his back pocket. He shook the box before turning it over in his hand as though he was looking at it for the first time. Slowly taking out a match and cupping his hands, he strikes the match before putting it to the bowl of his pipe and sucks hard. The bowl of the pipe glowed red, then seemed to die. Taking it out of his mouth he looks at it hard. Satisfied, he put it back into his mouth, sat back and sucks again at the end of the stem.

'Was it Barry Lake who was stabbed?' I take a sip from my half pint and look at the other tables, where a few people had sat and were discussing the menu.

'Bacon burger...'

'Fancy chicken and chips...'

'The ribs look tasty...'

'Those salads sound great...'

I turn back to the old man. '... possibly, it's a long time ago now,' he says looking at his now empty glass, then at me, looking at the glass then gently rolling it round on its base.

Taking the hint, I picked up his glass, asking, 'What did you have?'

Someone from another table said, 'Just tell Alice it's for young John.'

'Young John?' I look towards the old man who just sat eyes closed to the sun.

'Yes, tell them over the bar it's for 'young John'.'

So, I go to the counter and asked for a refill for 'Young John'. The amused barmaid fills the glass. 'He usually has a bacon butty, just hang on a bit, I think it's ready?'

A pint *and* a bacon butty? Might get a story though. I rock back and forth on my heels as I wait.

In short time I am placing the pint and the butty down in front of 'young John'.

'Ta!' He puts down his pipe before taking a dubiously clean hankie out of his pocket to wrap his teeth in, placing hankie with teeth by his pipe before picking up the butty. 'They do the best bacon butty round these parts.' Looking at my nearly half empty glass, he continues, 'Did you not buy one for yourself?'

I shake my head. 'The stabbing,' I say, with just a little frustration beginning to graze the words. 'You were going to tell me about the stabbing.' I obviously needed to wait till he had eaten his butty without teeth. Perhaps they should have cut the crusts off. No wonder his lips seemed to protrude a bit. I sigh then had another sip of my now warm beer.

Finishing off his butty and taking a long sip, he says, 'Yeah, it was Barry Lake.'

I had drifted off listening to others' conversations. 'Do you remember Peter getting up the…' much laughter, 'bout his girl-friend, what's her name…?' I turn my head swiftly towards Young John. 'Sorry!'

'Got to keep up young'un. Barry Lake was stabbed in January. January had lots of snow.' He nods his head as he returns yet again to study his pipe.

'How did Barry come to be stabbed?'

I swallow the last of my beer.

'Don't know.'

I sit still in disbelief for several moments. 'You don't know?'

'It snowed in January. Not here in January.'

'You said you had chestnuts in January?'

'Yeah, did have chestnuts in January. Good chestnuts they were.'

'But you were not here…' I tap the bench forcibly, 'here in the pub?'

'No,' he puffs on his pipe, 'Snowed in January. Had chestnuts at home in me grate.'

I sigh, looking round the now full garden. I finish the last dregs of my beer. 'It has been good to see you John.'

'Good of you to buy me lunch young man. Sure you'll go far.'

Standing, I turn to see my boss with a furious look on his face walking towards me.

'Why are you here?' he shouted.

'You said to come here!' I reply in frustration.

'No I didn't!' Stabbing his finger in my chest. 'I told you 'The Old Oak at Leeming' and I find you here chatting to my dad!' He drops his hand and more to himself he mutters, 'And I thought you were bright.'

Head bowed, feeling a total fool, I walk quickly to my little Mini.

Opening the car door, I hear Young John shout, 'Now, now son, not so 'arsh else I'll tell him what you did!'

'Don't you dare!' came the angry retort.

Quickly I get in the car, seat belt on with engine running. I glance in their direction to catch them glaring at each other, then pull the motor away with a grin, wondering 'What did he do that his dad could threaten him with?' As I pull out of the carpark, 'Now that would make a much better story – if I dare!'

This story was inspired by a 29-year-old who died on the streets of Bognor in 2017, as there were no places available for her in a night shelter. So, Louise, this is in memory of you.

What I Miss

I am laying on some covers, now tattered and torn. I no longer notice the smell of them, as I probably smell more. Not yet has darkness descended. There are people still about. A sandwich of something, half eaten is being put down. A half empty cup of Coke or similar stood alongside. Do they not realise I am still a person, resting on my side? Not all are like that, I must say now. An elderly lady, finding walking difficult, left me cleansing wipes while she thought I slept. I was huddled out of the cold, which seeped in below my feet.

A right strange couple, bible people, who purse their lips at me. It's OK for them, I think, they are going home for tea. I miss the smell of freshly bought bread, I miss the smell of freshly baked cake. I miss the smell of home, more than most would think. Life was going well, then trouble beckoned. Now I don't belong.

An elderly gent bent almost in half, swallowing before he could speak, sat beside me on Tuesday, careful to leave his walking stick out of harm's way. He chewed his cheek, his lips, and looked at the sun. 'You should not be too bad today; they say it will be warmer.'

'Warmer than what?' I wonder, as he struggles up on his feet, leaving some coins where he'd sat. He didn't realise most places would not let me through their doors! I can see my granny's kitchen with its stove in the corner heating water. Everything combustible goes into the stove to 'make coal go further'. Life was good, then trouble beckoned, and now I don't belong.

It might be sunny, but winter is here. The bitter wind blows down the freezing pavements, getting worse as day turns to night. I huddle further down in my covers, drag my feet up to keep them warmer. No food to eat tonight, but I half dream of a night out with mates. We were noisy, drank too much. Ate too much and pushed dessert down even though we had no room. We laughed our way out of town, not caring who we disturbed. Life was good then, and now I don't belong.

People hurrying, Christmas is coming, their laughter shrieking through the cold night air. The noise my poor ears cannot stand, my throat is raw. I cannot swallow. A nicely dressed lady gives me a hot drink, holding my head while I sip. My eyes were too blurred to care, but she remained till the last drop went down. Then she covered up my head. I don't remember her leaving, but slept till early morning. Her body sat close with another hot drink to slip down my throat. I dream of Mum, her hand on my head, tutting slightly. She raised my head, lemon and honey was her medicine. It was always in the cupboards, came out for all head colds. She would place hot water bottles at my feet, leave the window open. Life was good then, and now I don't belong.

I wake up at dawn, my saviour no longer here. My feet burned, not used to heat. The hot water bottle gone. My toes are turning black, I look at my fingers, then put them in my armpits hoping for a semblance of warmth. I watch the street cleaners and the toilet cleaners going about their tasks. Their thick boots and warm socks are mostly all I see. I remember my old Dad going out in similar style. I used to laugh at him; he'd shake his head at me before he closed the door. He was a night watchman, Mum made him up a food tin. Life was good then, and now I no longer belong.

The days get shorter, colder, wetter. I no longer feel my feet, my hands or face. I find I cannot hear nor keep my eyes open. I stay here, I lay and wait. I drift off into a land I can only dream of, a land of hope, of light and warmth. I think I smile, my mouth is frozen, but I focus on the light. I no longer hear the footsteps, hurrying or shuffling past. I see not the shoes nor think of memories past. I no longer worry about food or drink. I follow the light because I know, at last, this is where I belong.

novum PUBLISHER FOR NEW AUTHORS

Rate
this **book**
on our
website!

www.novum-publishing.co.uk

HERZ FÜR AUTOREN A HEART FOR AUTHORS À L'ÉCOUTE DES AUTEURS MIA KAPΔIA ΓIA ΣYΓΓP
HJÄRTA FÖR FÖRFATTARE UN CORAZÓN POR LOS AUTORES YAZARLARIMIZA GÖNÜL VERELIM SZÍ
CUORE PER AUTORI ET HJERTE FOR FORFATTERE EEN HART VOOR SCHRIJVERS TEMOS OS AUTO
SZÍVÜNKÉRT SERCE DLA AUTORÓW EIN HERZ FÜR AUTOREN A HEART FOR AUTHORS À L'ÉCOU
CORAÇÃO BCEЙ ДУШОЙ K ABTOPAM ETT HJÄRTA FÖR FÖRFATTARE Á LA ESCUCHA DE LOS AUTO
AUTEURS MIA KAPΔIA ΓIA ΣYΓΓPAΦEIΣ UN CUORE PER AUTORI ET HJERTE FOR FORFATTERE EEN
YAZARLARIMIZA GÖNÜL VERELIM SZÍVÜNKÉRT SERCE DLA AUTORÓW EIN HERZ FÜR
VOOR SCHRIJVERS TEMOS OS AUTORES CORAÇÃO BCEЙ ДУШОЙ K ABTOPAM ETT HJÄRTA FÖ

The author

Having had a varied career, mainly in office work,
Bee Grey moved from Hayes to Nottingham, where
she helped to run a small post office. It was here
that Bee became familiar with computers, and as
such an opportunity arose to teach adults about
Microsoft Windows. She took this opportunity
and continued in this role until she retired to the
South Coast with her husband, Eric. Bee came
to writing late in life, as she is dyslexic and found
that computers were helpful in this pursuit when
she eventually obtained one. She enjoys reading,
writing, and knitting for charity.

novum 📖 PUBLISHER FOR NEW AUTHORS

The publisher

*He who stops
getting better
stops being good.*

This is the motto of novum publishing, and our focus
is on finding new manuscripts, publishing them and
offering long-term support to the authors.
Our publishing house was founded in 1997, and since
then it has become THE expert for new authors and
has won numerous awards.

**Our editorial team will peruse each manuscript
within a few weeks free of charge and without
obligation.**

You will find more information about
novum publishing and our books on the internet:

www.novum-publishing.co.uk